The Devil's Trill

HAUNTED REQUIEMS

The Devil's Trill

Lyra R. Saenz

4 Horsemen
Publications, Inc.

4 Horsemen
Publications, Inc.

4 Horsemen Publications, Inc.
1497 Main St. Suite 169
Dunedin, FL 34698
4horsemenpublications.com
info@4horsemenpublications.com

Typeset by Michelle Cline
Edited by Jen Paquette

Library of Congress Control Number: 2022944617

Print ISBN: 979-8-8232-0025-7
Audio ISBN: 979-8-8232-0023-3
Ebook ISBN: 979-8-8232-0024-0

Table of Contents

Content Warnings

This novella contains spoilers for *Sonata*, book 2 of Lyra R. Saenz's Nocturne Symphony. Readers who have not yet read *Sonata* are advised to pause before venturing further.

Additional Warnings: Mentions of rape, torture, domestic abuse, stillbirth/infanticide, and abortion.

'Til Death Do Us Part...

There are secrets between lovers,
So very dark and ugly.
We'll take them to our graves one day,
where the dirt stinks of decay.

But secrets never die.
Not really.
Not for some.
For all your deeds come out to play until
secrets there are none.

I married my love's secrets.
I wear them on my neck,
Where fingers wound and wrapped
and wrung,
Until I could not take breath.

There are secrets between lovers,
so dirty, dank, and grim.
We lay them in our marriage bed,
to rest with sacred vim.

But parasites don't sleep.
They dine on us instead.
They nibble at our toes,
Grow fat upon our souls.

They grow and grow and grow some more,
Until there's no more left to eat.

Lyra R. Saenz

CHAPTER 1

The Overture

I saw death in her eyes.

I saw it plainly as I see you reading this page. It was not a threat, nor even a promise. It simply was. I was going to die, and I was so sure she was going to be the cause, I lost sight of the real war instead. I fought, of course. I fought like hell, but how can you fight fate when you're blind to the future?

I was going to die, and I thought I stood before my executioner.

Turns out, the ax swung from below.

IT SMELLS LIKE SHIT. ALL DUNGEONS SMELL like shit, even the most high-tech ones. Excuse me, prisons... All *prisons* smell like shit. Gotta be politically correct. "Dungeons" is too medieval—whatever that's supposed to account for. Not that the change in designation actually accounts for anything. Clean and sterile and shiny with its chromium plated bars, glass doors, ID scanners and automated security systems, yet it smells like human feces left out in the heat for five days before someone scooped it up, put it in a pot, and mixed in the breast sweat of a six-ton elephant who hasn't left the stable in over a year to make stew: a *creme de la poopoo*. That's what it smells like here. Hard-boiled shit.

Not that I can say it's unexpected. I mean, what else are you supposed to write with in here? Well, that's what the lycans and vampyres use anyway.

I don't get even that luxury.

Creatures like me aren't afforded the same meager accommodations as more mundane hexen. We're too ... how do you say ... unpredictable.

"Put the witch in for holding. The general will decide what to do with her later."

Witch... That's me. My designation, my title, my number... the witch. To think I would be living the high life in Lorelei surrounded by my army of chimera were it not for those infantile technomancers.

Meddlesome brats!

My cell is made of the finest titanium. Six perfectly identical sides to make a pristine cube, I wouldn't be able to tell which direction was up or down were it not for gravity keeping me upright, and every panel is laced with anti-magic tech. The silver-laced wires pulse with a dull white light. (Were I to so much as look at them wrong, they'd light up and load me up with enough voltage to down a water buffalo.) There is no bed, just a raised slab. At first glance, I thought it was made of the same hard steel as the walls, but the first time I sat in it, it yielded to my weight. When I sleep, it shapes itself to my body, a perfect cloud of comfy. It would be a five-star experience were it not for the fact that it radiates a disturbing field of hot/cold energy whenever I lie there. A massage with too much and too little pressure designed to subdue anyone who lays their corpse in it. It makes for a fitful sleep, hard to wake from and disturbingly easy to fall into.

One Star.

Out of curiosity, I once tried to fling myself against the wall in an effort to bash my own miserable head in, but just like the "bed," the structure yielded, and I ended up bounced unceremoniously onto my ass like a five-year-old in a balloon house. Heh... and they say we bend the laws of reality. What have they to say for what they warp with their science? Walls shouldn't have the surface tension of a trampoline one moment only to harden to solid stone the next.

And the waste room situation... a square bowl welded to the floor. Imagine if you will, the way a dog has to squat to pee only it's wearing a short dress and heels and its front paws are tied together... That's how I feel every time I use it regardless of my lack of proper footwear. Just something about the angle and position makes me have to lift my heels a good five inches to aim properly. Because they don't want me getting creative with my bodily fluids (witches can get a lot done with a little urine and the right array), my waste bin is monitored by several droids and emptied the moment it is soiled. I made the mistake of trying to go outside my little bowl, once. We won't talk about how that ended.

Definitely leaving a negative review on this stay.

As if merely using the cursed toilet and bed weren't difficult enough, cameras follow my every sneeze and fart. They keep me in manacles: pretty steel bracelets linked to one another with a cord of radioactive something or other. I don't know what exactly the material is, but it makes me so tired I can barely wake up more than the two or three times a day they feed me, and that's only because they turn the damn things off so I can move around without accidentally strangling myself. Speaking of... Why don't they just let me strangle myself? What could they want with a live witch? I was under the impression the League wanted us eradicated, not living the shit-scented high life in one of their resort prisons.

Without windows or clocks, I can only judge how long I've been here by the number of meals brought to me. I estimate, if they are being stingy, that it's been a little more than a week. I've never gone so long without using magic, and I can feel my powers festering.

It's an achy, uncomfortable feeling: magical atrophy.

You know how when people end up bedridden, their muscles atrophy. The muscles deteriorate, they lose their ability to move around, so their skin builds up bedsores, and after the physical body has had enough, the mind just kind of goes a little lopsided. That's what it feels like when a witch doesn't use her magic. It festers inside like ants dying under the skin, and no matter how much you scratch, the itch only worsens until...

ACCESS GRANTED

The A.I. attached to my cell's locking mechanism chimes over the intercom in a cheery singsong voice. Why do these +ies always choose feminine voices for their artificial intelligence?

"Well, well, well... Look what we have here."

The man that walks into my cell is more machine than person: a robotic arm, half his face metal and bolted in place, the shine of silver under his shirt collar, and by the resonant echo of his right boot, he's got himself a prosthetic leg, too. The few fleshy parts I can see seem knitted together with wire cabling and scar tissue. When he looks at me with muddy green eyes, the hair at the back of my neck rises.

"What do you want?" I spit out as I find my feet. Like hell I'm going to keep lounging on my back as a technomancer invades my cozy little stink pit.

"The boys told me you were a freak, but they mention how easy you were on the eyes."

His eyes... Goddess below! I've met serpents with more human eyes. Human in biology they may be but they are monstrous in intention.

"Stay away from me."

"Just relax, witchy."

"Guards!" I call. He laughs.

"Really now? Who do you think let me in here?"

He reaches for me with his mechanical hand. On impulse, I lash out with my magic, trying with all my might to summon something to my defense, but nothing comes. Not even a puff of smoke. It merely lingers, hollow at my fingertips like cobwebs.

Pain flairs in my cheek as he slaps me across the face with enough force to send me nose-first into the wall. Cold digits close around the nape of my neck and my feet leave the floor.

"Let go of me—ah!"

The wall punches the air from my lungs. It's cold against my front. I kick backward; my bare heel hits his metal leg. Ouch! White pain zings up my leg.

"Come on, love. I promise I'll show you a good time."

Eyes closed: teeth gritted... *Is this really happening right now?*

"Montwyatte!"

Everything stops. The world grinds to a halt and suddenly my heart isn't racing as fast anymore. The hands leave my body. My damaged foot can't hold my weight, so I slump to my knees. It's definitely broken ... or at least sprained. Goddamn cyborgean arseholes.

"Well, if it isn't the flunky. What do you want, Donnie? Scared I won't leave anything for you?"

My hair is tangled in the bolts that make up the joints of his fingers.

"Miss Helsdottir will not to be treated in such a manner. She is considered an asset to the state, and I advise you to leave these premises now."

The new entrant is by the door, obstructed from my view. I can only see a pair of polished dress shoes under the hem of a pair of finely pressed black slacks, but his voice is soothing, like warmed butter over cinnamon toast. There's a gliding rhythm to it, the kind of voice that should be reciting poetry over an open campfire while bongos play on the outskirts and naturalists pass the devil's grass back and forth. Who is this man?

"Or what, Donnie-boy? You'll tell daddy on me?"

My would-be rapist huffs like a spoiled teenager caught sneaking his girlfriend into his dormitory. I'm noticing now the notches on the back of his neck: lines of ink of varying widths all in a column along his cervical spine. It reminds me of the olden days when the hexen royals used to tattoo sigils on non-magical humans as a means to keep track of them and any augmentations they undertook. The sigils would connect them to a psionic witch capable of tracking their every thought, word, and deed for disloyalty or dissent. Suffice to say, this was just one of the reasons the human+ revolted.

Maybe if the psionics had done their job right, we wouldn't be in this mess...

Only, this tattoo isn't even remotely one of those sigils, or if it is, it's been deconstructed into a series of lines tik-tac-toe-ing across the man's back. I wonder if each line represents something, like notches on a bedpost, or maybe the tattoo as a whole has a meaning of its own.

"I would ask you not to call me that."

"Or what, short stuff?"

"Last I checked, despite my lack of technomancer certification, I outrank you during wartime."

"'During wartime,' he says. Hah! What a joker! Wartime, my ass."

The man laughs his way past the other male and out the door. The air trapped in my lungs escapes, a long sigh of relief I didn't even know I was holding. The room feels so much bigger now that his mass is gone from the space. I take the moment to breathe.

In... 2... 3... 4... Out... 2... 3... 4... In... 2...

"Are you alright?"

The hand hovering before me is well-manicured. A heavy signet ring decorates his index finger. The sleeve of his shirt is held by a silver cufflink adorned with a single opal. It's a nice-looking hand. One I wouldn't mind taking.

"I'll be fine."

His palm is cool to the touch, his grip firm but not too tight.

"Good. That's very good. My name is Donarick."

Wow... Looking into his eyes, one mechanical, one human, something slides into place that I didn't even know was askew. It's jarring, being confronted by your own incompletion, your own shortcomings. Worst of all, it makes me dizzy, this new feeling.

I've never fallen up before.

CHAPTER 2
War March

If there was one lesson I learned as a child that I think stands true today, it's that creatures like me either live forever or die young.

S o I join Seraphim's forces in exchange for my freedom, not that I really have much choice. Either fight or rot away in my little titanium cell. It's a sweet deal really. I get to kill as many human+ as I want, and in return, no one bothers me ever again. I'm not sure whose idea it was to recruit hexen to their cause, but I've got to hand it to them: technomancers and witches working side by side to bring down a common enemy? It's brilliant!

I don't think too highly of the Pontiflex Catalan or General Llywellyn. They're no different than any other power-hungry politician I've ever heard of. Greedy old men are greedy old men no matter their creed or color.

The Pontiflex's son, on the other hand, is a conundrum. Donarick Thames is no technomancer. He failed his examinations last year, and I don't expect he'll ever truly pass. He lacks a proper understanding of what it means to use techno-magic. Besides, he's too kind. I see him running negotiations back and forth like an eager puppy between the Pontiflex and the old Goblin King, Yggfret. Yes, I stand amidst the last true hexen royalty. Yggfret Bloodfang is even more intimidating in person than his reputation gives him credit for, yet he indulges the young adept like a butcher fattening up a prize hog.

"I shall be venturing with the general's forces as they march on Deriva."

Yggfret's declaration comes as a surprise to all of us gathered in the "special" accommodations Seraphim's military has provided us in their radiation-poisoned wilderness. (Goddess forbid, we let the witches stay within the actual city limits where radiation filters keep the masses safe from the nuclear waste their own government created.) He is the only one who is here willingly. Something about having negotiated our release in a bargain with the Pontiflex. Every one of us has been rotting on the inside of a cell for some length of time. You can tell based on the decrepit state of us all. If you ask me, the only marked improvement between this bunker and my prison cell is the added bunk beds. And I suppose the smell is slightly better, less hard-boiled and stale than *l'odeur de merde*.

"Why for? They don't need us."

While the other witches granted freedom in exchange for service are just as eager to spill +ie blood, they don't trust our newfound allies as far as they can throw them, and for some of us like Monsieur Géant, who boasts inhuman strength, that can be pretty far. I'm not sure if it's his naturally strong will or the leftover influence of giant blood that makes him so critical of Yggfret, but the goblin king seems just about ready to eat the half-giant witch himself.

"There is something I need to verify in Deriva. When better a time than when our allies march against it?"

"And if they fail?" inserts the bruja Xochtli. Short in stature but not in presence, the woman's voice, thick with an old Mestizo accent, echoes about the room in the voices of other witches.

"Then they fail. Their failure has no bearing on my venture."

Even if we are presently in alignment with Seraphim, we have no confidence in them or their ability to win a war against the rest of the continent. After all, why would they seek the help of witches if they were capable of making change themselves? Surely, it isn't just a neighborly show of faith.

Seraphim, as the northernmost country in Deus, is the closest neighboring country to the Wastes. The last major hexen territory, the Wastes have become something of a boogeyman to humans, a place where monsters and horrors abound. I've never been personally. I was too busy being raised in an orphanage amidst a bunch of humans who would've tossed me out on the street the moment they realized what I was. That far into the center of the continent, Hexen-led territories like the Wastes were a distant dream. Well, until I met another hexen child. He used to speak of the Wastes as though they were some far-off utopia where all hexen could live a full life, free from the woes of human+ society. Whispered stories in the night long after lights out. We'd sit and fantasize about the wilds, about running away together to find the Wastes. Ah... Those were wonderful nights. He was the one who first taught me how to control my magic. He swore after he came of age and found his freedom from our little patch of hell that he would whisk me away like some knight in shining armor. I would have loved that.

Alas, a week before his coming of age, one of the overseers caught him fiddling with a spell. He disappeared the next day. Nothing was said about his absence, just that the orphanage decided to let him leave early. That's all: a quiet steal into the night. I didn't believe it, and I never saw him again.

Two years later, when I came of age, I summoned a salamander into the electrical room. We weren't allowed matches, and most buildings are fireproof anyway—at least against mundane fires. Magical flame, on the other hand... Suffice to say the whole building burned down within minutes, and I made sure to barricade the emergency exits so the adults couldn't get out. I thought I would make my way to the Wastes after but ended up in Lorelei instead.

Now, I'm here, watching and waiting for the country who will "unify" the continent to commence with said unification. Apparently, Deriva is the initial domino that must crumble for it all to work.

"What's in Deriva, Yggfret?"

The witch king's mouth twists into a sadistic sneer.

"Let's just say I owe the Vulcana a visit."

Right. The Vulcana, the technomancer Elisabeta De Claré. She's the one who took off part of his left ear. Her quick-fire son and smart-mouthed stepdaughter are the reason I'm even part of this poor excuse for a coup. (Che! This whole thing is doomed to fail. Seraphim has the fewest technomancers on their roster.)

"You'd best make arrangements for your own accommodations, Yggfret," says Xochtli. "I doubt our new 'friends' will manage anything considerable."

What could motivate Seraphim to attack Deriva of all places first? Deriva is a fairly neutral island country. Did the Vulcan do something to upset the Pontiflex? I smell a vendetta, or is there some resource they want: use of their navy, access to a port and the goods kept a plenty there, or is it something else? But they couldn't. Seraphim doesn't have the muscle or the resources to go up against any of the other League nations.

"W-w-what if th-they s-s-s-succeed?" asks a mousy looking fellow in the back.

What then, indeed? Well, we go to war, obviously. It'll be the war to end all wars. Technomancers vs. technomancers. The destruction! Our ancestors vacated earth to escape a nuclear winter. Did we really go through all of that trouble just to allow Deus to fall to the same fate?

The witch who asks the question shakes under Yggfret's gaze. I would've thought him to be a shifter were it not for the indicia burning orange at his nose: a strange little mouse done in a single stroke. He must have an attunement to animals, particularly rodents if the rat seated on his shoulder is any indication. He's been whispering back and forth with it for the last hour, and this is the first time he's said anything loudly enough to be heard by human ears. This is hardly the kind of witch who should be on the front lines of a world war. What did he do to end up in a prison cell? Faint wrong in the street? Pathetic creature.

"They won't," scoffs Géant.

"They m-m-might," squeaks the rat-tamer.

"Yes, and one day a basilisk will lay a chicken egg so it can hatch into a pixie bear."

The whole room chimes with laughter at Géant's shrewd joke, including Yggfret who can't help but chuckle into his fist. Yes, we're all here enjoying fine wine and military hospitality at the behest of a country none of us feel has a chance to win. How could they? They couldn't even pass any technomancers at this last year's trials.

"You may yet find yourself a pixie bear, Géant, and not too long from now if my stars are right."

"What do you know, Yggfret?"

"Divination has always been my favored art."

"Divination is a load of stargazing crock. You and I both know no one can truly tell the future."

"And yet here I am, the willing guest of a League country about to stage a coup d'etat against its allies. What do you take me for? A halfwit like you who got yourself caught stealing from an airship?"

"At least I was doing something to disrupt the +ies. Meanwhile, you sit in a hovel hole on the side of a mountain—"

"Géant!" inserts Xochtli. "Have a care. You'd still be drawing sigils with your piss were it not for Yggfret!"

"If it weren't for Yggfret, I'd be ringing your neck, you worm-encrusted—"

I've no idea who throws the first spell, but a god-awful staticky sound falls from Xochtli's mouth at the same time Géant throws his fist. This! This is the reason witches are rapidly losing the war against the League. We can't work together. We're too volatile on our own. Put too many of us in a room together and chances are the room won't survive. Really, if we ever want to reclaim our status as the royalty of this wretched continent, someone will have to figure out how to get us all to work together.

A blast of fire singes the tips of my horns. I grit my teeth and summon magic to my fingertips. Should we summon a banshee or a gorgon? The banshee would out-scream everyone and shut the whole room up, while the gorgon would just turn everyone to stone, thus achieving the same result.

I could just flip a magical coin. Yes, a random magical weave sounds chaotic enough.

Before I even begin the summoning, the buzzer over the doorway goes off.

"Ladies and gentlemen, please. There's no need for dissent. We are all here under the same banner."

It's Donarick. Dressed exactly as he came to me two days before, the human+ stands with his hands clasped in front of his waist in a pose reminiscent of an opera singer. Are you here to give us an aria, dear Thames?

"Well, if it isn't our generous host," sneers Géant.

"I understand the change in your circumstances might be difficult to digest," comes Donarick's response. "But I promise you full autonomy outside of these walls should you choose to vacate them."

"Full autonomy doesn't guarantee safety from your adepts, borg," says Xochtli. "You honestly think we trust you enough to simply wander about unguarded?"

"Perhaps not, but you are in full possession of your magics. You have my full permission to act in self-defense should one of our people act in defiance of their orders. They are expected to treat you as honored allies. Our war efforts depend on our mutual trust."

"Your war efforts, more like, and what happens when your people end up running away with their tails between their legs?"

"I assure you, Monsieur Géant, we will win."

"That a fact?"

"Consider it a promise, my friend."

Donarick's mechanical eye glows a bloody red as he utters these words. I find myself wondering if he has ever actually been in battle before. Has he killed before? If so, how many? Has he even shed blood before? Someone so clean has to have killed at least once. I've never met a human+ capable of soothing a room of hexen.

"Miss Helsdottir, could I have a moment?"

All eyes turn to me. Yggfret's mouth holds an intrigued quirk. I may not know the witch personally, but I know enough about him not to read into it. There's too much there to examine.

"Sure…"

"Outside if that is alright? I have a filtration mask for you that should fit perfectly."

Really? I think as he slides his own mask back over his face. Outside in the nuclear frost? What does he need to speak of that can't be done in the comfort of our homely little witch barracks?

Donarick's hand is extended toward me. His smile is kind even if it only reaches one eye. I don't take his hand, but I do follow him out the door.

It's cold outside. It was still hot as can be farther south when I was imprisoned. One month later and were I any farther south, winter would still be a figment of my imagination. Not here though. While winter inches forward at a drunken snail's pace for the rest of the continent, it is already in full fury here. There may not be snow on the ground, but make no mistake, this place is as chilled as a meat freezer. Icicles hang off the edges of the gutters, and the trees are as barren as can be. Even the pines have lost their needles, though I doubt that is due to any kind of chill.

Even through the safety gear the adept handed me as we stepped out the door, the cold bites my nose and nips at my ears. Radiation masks aren't the most insulated, and evil be blessed, I sweat like a pig whenever I wear one. Never mind that the smell of rubber and self-healing glass is absolutely abhorrent. If I focus on it too much, my horns ache at the sudden shift in temperature. Inside, the furnace was cranked high enough to melt the wax off a candle.

"As much as I love traipsing around in a toxic wasteland, I'm rather confused as to why this conversation must take place amidst the elements."

"My apologies, Miss Helsdottir," he says, continuing along the path. "But if this meeting goes as I hope, we will have need of the space."

Oh...

We round the side of the next complex and a barren beachside comes into view, rocky, more mud than sand, and half-frozen as summer leaves the rest of the continent. I've seen the view before. I saw it when they transported me from my prison cage to my new shared accommodations. This particular stretch of sea makes a crescent moon inlet into the land. A few gulls poke their beaks into the sand searching for crabs. They find litter instead: bottle caps, aluminum tins, bullet shells. My lip curls in disgust. Damned human+, thinking the earth is theirs to pollute and contaminate with no regard for how their actions will one day destroy everything worth saving in this place.

Something new to the view, however, is the large enclosure now closing off the channel which leads out to open water and framing the entirety of the beach. Dotted along the fencing are several adepts, all wearing hazmat suits and sporting electrical prongs as though awaiting the opportunity to shock some large animal into submission.

"Making new accommodations for us?" I jeer.

"To come to the point, I would like to request your might on our expedition to Deriva. I feel your unique skill set will prove quite valuable on this upcoming raid."

"My unique skill set?"

"Your ability to summon monsters."

"Netherbeasts."

Not monsters. Monsters are a different thing entirely.

"Yes, netherbeasts. There is one in particular that I feel would be very useful on this venture. You wouldn't by chance have the ability to summon and control a cipactli into this paddock?"

"A what?"

"Cipactli. The legendary sea monster whose body was used to create the Old-World continents of Latin and South America. Have you heard of it?"

"Do I look like a descendant of the Aztecs to you?" I spit, gesturing to my pale skin and too-red hair. Last name is Helsdottir for crying out loud.

"The cipactli of legend was a part of the Aztec and Mayan creation myths. Part crocodile, fish, and toad. Tezcatlipoca used his own foot as bait to lure the creature out of the water and kill it. From its body, they made the earth. If you need an image for your imagination, by all means, take a look."

The hologram Donarick pulls up would be comical, at best—an overgrown fish with a crocodilian mouth and the hind legs of a toad—were it not for the extra jaws decorating the beast's body. Teeth... Teeth everywhere, that would be the better description for such a beast. I can only imagine what it would be like to fight such a creature. Did you manage to avoid the head? Yes... whelp, too bad! The tail took a big bite out of your arse. Oh, you avoided the tail too? No worries, not only did you get slashed by the front claw, but the gnashing jaws on its palm have eaten your spleen.

"So let me get this straight. You want me to summon a legendary netherbeast that was allegedly killed by a god? How is that supposed to help anything?"

"There's more than one," Donarick explains. "And legendary isn't so much a descriptor as it is a misnomer. You can't expect indigenous cultures to understand how dimensional travel works."

"Right," I drawl out. I've never summoned a cipa-whatever-the-damned-thing-is-called, so chances of me being able to control it are slim to none. "Well, thanks but no thanks. I don't feel like losing a foot today."

Not for you. Not for any augmented person on the face of this godforsaken planet.

"Tezcatlipoca lost more than a measly foot trying to kill that singular beast. But not to worry, I promise your safety is of the highest priority."

He has no idea what kind of consequences can arise from a misaligned summoning. I could summon the wrong thing, pull myself into a wormhole, cause a dimensional riff, or if by some miracle I am successful, I would be perfectly primed to act as the creature's next meal.

"Your promises don't amount to jack-didly-squat in the face of a netherbeast."

"Then allow me to provide you with some insurance."

There's something hidden in his statement that doesn't sit well with me. He gestures to the side and a pair of guards step out of the vehicle. Between them, they drag along a limp-bodied woman. Judging from the scaly tail dragging the ground and the smoothed features of her face, I would imagine she is a hexen. One of the lizardfolk who thrive in the abandoned sewage of radiation dampened cities.

"I realized you would be reluctant to put yourself in danger, so I thought we'd appease your summoning with some dinner ahead of time."

Ignorant fool.

"You think one measly sacrifice is going to appease an angry netherbeast known for ripping the foot off of a god?"

"Perhaps not, but my men are ready to pull you out and trap the beast the moment it enters this plane."

"Where it gets its next meal from is the least of my concern. I've never summoned anything bigger than a displacer beast." And that blasted creature wouldn't obey a word I said even when I had my athame. Without it, I haven't a hope of summoning anything stronger than a forest nisse. "Perhaps, you don't mind having your head ripped off by an uncontrollable netherbeast, but I would rather not venture the risk."

Oh, look, one of the buzzards found a bottle top in the sand. Two of its compatriots have decided its superior shine is deserving of a contest of will. They squawk and peck at each other until their oh-so-coveted prize goes hurtling into the water.

"Perhaps this might help."

My brow furrows as he beckons one of his men over. The guard presents to Donarick a long, thin box warded with magic suppressing tech nodes. Donarick tip-taps some sort of code into the box's side and the nuts and bolts that make up the casing unwind like clockwork. It reminds me of a girl I used to know at the orphanage. She had one prized possession that she would never let anyone touch: a jewelry box with a swan lake ballerina nestled within. I used to love watching the ballerina spin to the rhythmic chimes of the music. I hated the way the last note never quite finished, leaving the whole composition hanging on a dissonant key. She said it was because she dropped it when the adepts rescued her from her burning home. All the jewelry spilled out, but she saved the box. It was the only thing besides her that made it out, including her parents in whose bedroom the fire began.

That girl was adopted not long after she arrived—go figure with her pretty blue eyes and skin as white as snow. I wonder if the last note ever played again.

There's no music coming out of this box though. Just dead silence.

As the lid lifts, a holographic shield pops up around the box, locking in place the outpouring of malignant energy. Settled within, nestled in the bedding of a silken cushion and leaking magic like a runny faucet, lies a carved length of wood. About as long as my forearm, the reddened wood is of simple yet elegant design, finely tapered and adorned with geometric carvings throughout the shaft. The grip is wound with cream-colored leather and bound with purple wax. But the physical attributes of the instrument, while pretty and worth taking note of, are not what beguile me so. The wand hums with power. Old power. The kind of power not even Yggfret could summon forth without some serious repercussions.

"I see I've captured your full attention. Allow me to introduce Dagslys—the Dawn Ripper."

At the mention of its name, the wand pulses a crimson red.

"Where did you get that?"

"Being the sole nuclear power in the League comes with its perks. You don't honestly think we are foolish enough to allow ancient magical artifacts to be left unaccounted for once their witches have been dealt with?"

"Whose was it?"

"The Seidr King Mørknatt."

"You're lying."

What young witch hasn't heard of Mørknatt? The last true king before Deus went to hell. The man summoned some of the greatest monsters and netherbeasts ever seen on this plane, and that's his wand. His wand! This wretched adept is holding the wand of the witch who brought dragons to Deus. I don't believe it.

Thames laughs as he shakes his head.

"Not at all. It took five full-fledged technomancers to bring him down. Of course, back in those days, we didn't have the same technologies we do now. I imagine two or three would do the trick today. No matter. He is gone but this lovely, little trinket remains. They tried to destroy it initially, but no one could put so much as a dent in it, so it's been sitting in the Vatidome's vault for nearly 600 years."

I don't know what the more appropriate reaction is: anger or awe.

"I didn't realize you people felt the need to gloat."

"I am not showing you this to gloat, Miss Helsdottir. Think of it more as an offering. This wand's owner was a summoner, just like you."

"So?"

"So... Perhaps you can gain mastery of it."

"And why would I want to do that?"

"It might give you just the boost you need to achieve the impossible."

"You think a wand that outlived its witch will listen to me!? Ha! You're battier than a vamp on a jolly rancher's blood!"

Donarick's lips twitch, one side into a smile, the other into a frown. Reminiscent of the time one of my caretakers had a stroke during lessons; one half of his face just stopped working. Only this doesn't seem necessarily involuntary... Could it be due to his augmentation?

"I have faith in you."

The wand pulses. Some witches experience magic like an auditory cue: humming, whining, and the like. Others have a more sensory response: it leaves an aftertaste on their tongue or builds like a stench in their noses. Others still have a physical response; it feels warm or cold or leaves gooseflesh along their arms. That's where I sit—in the physical camp. Only, mine is not so innocent.

I feel the power dripping off of the wand, and arousal flares in my belly.

Lust for power... unquenchable, inconsolable, and as deeply rooted in my magical system as the blood that flows through my heart. Most people crave skin or food or even pain. I *want* that wand.

"I can't make any promises," I tell him. "But I'll see what I can manage."

"We march on Deriva in one week. I'm hoping I can count on you to join our forces."

Hope all you want, Thames. Magical artifacts aren't computers. You can't just push a button and make them work.

"You must be joking. It takes an incredibly skilled magic user to claim the allegiance of another witch's artifact, and next to that, you want me to summon some legendary beast that I haven't even heard of. What are you playing at? Giving them an excuse to put me back in the pit?"

"Not at all. I may not fully understand the magnitude of what I am asking, but I do grasp the skill necessary to do it. That's why I pushed to have you pulled out of prison despite your youth."

I get it. So, there was a chance I would be left to rot were it not for my proven skillset. How grand!

"And what if I fail?"

His expression falters. So too does his steady grip on the wand's case, but before I can truly read into his countenance, the suave male visage is back and cranked up a few notches.

"Summer," he takes ahold of my hand, "I'm giving this to you because I believe you are the only one capable of it. I believe in you, Miss Helsdottir."

He believes in me. No one has ever told me they believe in me before. It's almost as titillating as the magic tickling my awareness. They say witches who lust over magic are the ones most likely to fall prey to magic fever and insanity.

They say lunacy ferments best in the sexual organs. They say witches who claim the lost artifacts of others are damned to the finite space between Hades and Limbo. They say... well, *they* say a lot of things. Most of it is bullshit.

As I reach for the wand, both sides of Donarick's mouth curve upward in a smile.

CHAPTER 3

Con Brio

I'm sure you think I had it coming. Hel, I think I had it coming.

ONE WEEK LATER - DERIVA
Nothing burns like void fire.

"Ahh!!!"

Prince Xipilli screams so nicely. It almost makes up for the last few weeks I spent sniveling in a cage because of him. Dagslys is quite apt at drawing blood even if it isn't quite meant for doing so yet. I've already made plans to reforge the wand into a blade. Something like my old athame, but it will probably need a longer hilt, and I'll need to make sure the core is compatible with the wood. After my first successful summoning, Donarick promised me he would begin setting up a crafting lab for me back in Vatidomus City.

"I don't know who you are, but I will make you pay for this."

Whomever trussed the poor boy up had enough sense to blindfold him before I came in here. Donarick said I could play with him all I wanted: my reward for helping bring down the capital of Deriva. There's a hissing sound behind me. Jormungandr is growing bored. The two-headed snake is no great world serpent now, barely the length of my arm, but there is enough venom in that bite to down a moose, and I'm sure I don't have to mention what happens when you look directly into the eyes of a basilisk, or rather, what happens when you look into the wrong set of eyes. His head with deathly gaze is practically asleep while his venomous head just continues to hiss, venom dripping down its maw.

"Aww, poor baby. All alone. No one is coming to save you. No daddy. No mummy. No big sister. Just you and me until we both die of boredom."

The wand tip sparks as I bring it to his chest once again, and the screams continue. The magic burns so nicely into his skin. The brand is almost complete, something to remember me by. The same rune that graces my throat, blown up and borned to his chest in a permanent scar. Every time he looks in the mirror, every time he takes a lover to bed, every time he goes to the beach, every moment he spends out in the open for anyone to see beneath that privileged royal collar will be one where they also see me. The thought fills me with so much glee, I can barely contain my laughter. Oh, I suppose he could go and get a skin graft to cover it up, or perhaps enough laser treatments will make it fade, but magical scarifications live beneath the skin. Even if he survives this experience, he'll need to constantly reapply a masking if he wants to banish it from his sight.

"Jormy, baby, why don't you keep our friend company while I check in on Lucy?"

The basilisk slithers from my arm to curl around the prince's torso and neck before seating itself at his head. The venom continues to drip slowly from the creature's fangs onto the man's forehead. I watch as the viscous fluid ambles its way down, between the crease of the man's eyebrows, past the bridge of his nose, and into the hollow points of his eyes. Once the droplet hits his tear ducts, the sizzling begins, and the prince thrashes in agony.

His screamed curses are music to my ears as I allow the door to slam shut behind me. I'll come back to collect Jormy in the morning.

Deriva really is a beautiful country. Most island countries are. There is just something about the way the sea nurtures the coast while the volcano's wrathful embers provide the impetus for new life to flourish. I've heard that the witches who once called Deriva home could manipulate lava the way others manipulate water, bending it to their will to harvest its healing and destructive properties. Those witches, contrary to the heated pool of power they controlled, were peace-loving pacifists who saw more terror in the eyes of their rage-filled goddesses than they ever would on the mortal plane. That's why they were exterminated so quickly. They didn't see any threat in the technomancers and were foolish enough to think they could live in peace with them.

They were wrong.

And did Pele or Xochitle come to their aid? No. The volcanic goddesses merely watched as their people were destroyed. After all, the volcano erupts at the behest of none.

Now, Deriva is controlled by technomancers. At least under the Moctezumo family, the islands have been kept clean, following strict legislature against pollution and waste. They even kept quotas on fishing and oil-harvesting in the oceans. Despite the "limitations," Deriva is the richest country in the League as far as oceanic resources go. It's unfortunate that Seraphim saw them as enemies: the high-browed fool of a Vulcan and his spitfire of a wife, now dead at the hands of my new allies. I shudder to think how much wildlife the nuclear pollution will kill and/or alter irrevocably. (Seraphim already destroyed its own land. Naturally, they'll destroy everyone else's.) I doubt there are enough hexen or fae left in the area to counter the effects of this war.

The sun is setting. There's something so picturesque about the way Ör shimmers red on the horizon. His reflection in the water is as bloody as the corpses that line the docks. I wonder how much of the stained water is from our great star and how much is actually blood in the water.

I didn't realize how late it was. I've been *visiting* with the young prince for over two hours.

A pair of soldiers rolls another body off the edge of the dock. They laugh as the corpse makes a heavy splash against the surface. I imagine the sharks will have quite the feast tonight.

"And they call us heathens..." I hush as I make my way out of the main compound and toward the beach. Here, all is as serene as ever. The violence didn't spill into this area. You would never think looking at this view that a massacre occurred just twenty meters away.

Ör finishes his descent. Purple overtakes the sky, and a few stars begin to twinkle. The moons aren't out. Or rather, they are, but there's a heavily black spot in the sky. One of the rare nights that Dei is dark, and Koi is in its new moon phase. They could be in an eclipse, but I don't care enough to look it up on the astronomy service. That would require the use of a computer or handheld, and the last time I handled anything even remotely high-tech was during a class I was forced to take at the orphanage. Three-hours a day for three weeks I was forced to learn how to type on an old-school keyboard. It was painful and annoying. The screen gave me a headache, the stress gave me indigestion, and I ended up with a rash along my hand and forearm. Needless to say, I dislike handling technology. I don't know why some witches are capable of handling tech willy-nilly while the rest of us can barely watch television for more than 30 minutes.

That's just the way things are.

The sand is warm under my toes. I've never been to the beach, before. It's kind of surreal that I stand here as a victorious raider just like my ancestors. Loki ought to be proud.

The waves crash steadily along the shore. Their constant sloshing is a calming repetition while their foamy crests glow in the darkness. Bioluminescent waves ... and just beyond that watery, rainbow array, my triumph.

Lucy, my cipactli, basks at the edge of the beach, letting the water rush over her scaly body. Like a great saltwater crocodile, she lies on her belly with her mouth open. Well, several of her mouths open. Her frog-like legs are extended behind her, twitching in the water. She used those limbs to jump the full length of Cresta de Corail not hours ago. It was her great maw that felled Tlanextli long enough for Llywellyn to slice the Vulcan's throat.

"Hey, baby girl, you doing okay?"

From the satchel at my side, I pull a nice treat for her and toss it. The speed with which her hind jaws clamp down on the arm is disturbing, and the two mouths at her back ankles tear into the meat with equal gusto. Her tail thrashes, whacking the water with great damp slaps loud enough to echo across the whole of the coastline.

I toss the entirety of the satchel to her. The crunching of bones and sinew fills the beach as she chows down on her treat.

"Good girl," I praise her, and she obediently slithers her way to me. That crocodilian maw, large enough to swallow me whole, nudges into my side. I take the invitation to wind my arms around her nose. I imagine if crocs could purr, she would be purring at the gentle touch of my hands on her snout. A piece of the Vulcan's sleeve is still caught between Lucy's teeth.

I wonder if Seraphim would have managed without my Lucy's might backing their nuclear weapons.

I barely met the deadline for departure.

It took me two days to attune Dagslys, another three to summon Lucy onto this plane, and another 32 hours before I fully had her under my thrall. It's no small feat to take command of a dead witch's magical artifact, but I did it. Two sleepless nights of exchanging magic with the wand, allowing it to pollute my system so my own power could in turn fuse to the instrument... It was a painful process, deliciously so.

Lucy's eyes, sunken into her head, would normally reflect a limey yellow in the low light, but under my influence, only a hollow blackness peers down at me. They are just like Jormy's eyes. The basilisk was an accidental summon, the second failure in my attempts to summon a cipactli. (The first beast... somewhere along the route from its dimension to ours... well, let's just say it came through compromised, for lack of a better word.) Jormungandr was so small, I thought the summoning had failed entirely until one of the adepts babysitting me keeled over after a bite to his ankle. A second made the mistake of swatting the snake away with a pole and got an eye-full of death. They would have killed him had I not interfered. Now, he's mine. My little two-headed baby. He's grown since, but it will be years before he reaches Lucy's size.

"How does it feel to be the witch who brought a country to its knees?"

Wearing a smirk I wouldn't call uncomely, Donarick stands at the edge of the brush-line where the walkway gives way to sand. What is he doing out here? Dressed down with only his camouflage trousers and a plain white button down, half undone and hanging loose around his hips, the man looks like the kind of subject a renaissance era sculptor might use as a model. He's no David, too slight of frame and not tall enough, but he might pass for a Mercury or Apollo with their nimble limbs and eternal youth.

"Shouldn't you be enjoying the celebration feasts with the other +ies?"

"I've no interest in eating at a dead man's table."

Lucy bristles at the intruder, a low growl rumbling up from her belly. I shush her away, and she belly-slides into the water with a hiss. Once her tail disappears, I turn toward the cyborg at the far side of the beach. I don't quite know what to make of this man yet. He has been kind to me, and not just in the moment when he kept that brute from attacking me in my cell, but ever since as well. After I acquiesced to taking Dagslys and summoning the cipactli, he had me moved into a wing of his father's private abode. He'd check in on me from time to time, make sure I was eating and sleeping alright, and there was even one memorable morning in which I woke up in the middle of the training studio where I'd accidentally fallen asleep while plotting summoning circles to find someone had moved me to the settee and thrown a blanket over me. I wonder if he moved me.

"I seem to recall you bragging at dinner the other day that the table we were eating upon once belonged to your great, great grandfather. Is that not eating at a dead man's table?"

"Yes, well… I find it distasteful to eat in a banquet hall when the corpse of the previous owner is still cooling in the rafters above your head."

Distasteful is an understatement. My nose wrinkles at the thought. Barbarians, the lot of them, supping below a fresh cadaver like animals who hang their kills in the trees for later.

"I guess you technomancers really aren't so different from us as you like to pretend you are."

"All is fair in war."

"You forgot love," I correct. "If you're going to quote poetry, at least do so correctly."

"Ah, my mistake. Allow me to rectify." He clears his throat. "'The rules of fair play do not apply in love and war.'"

"Hmm, I've never heard it that way before."

"Lyly's *Euphues: The Anatomy of Wit*. I found it to be a dated read, but some aspects of the text are timeless."

A snooty little literature snob, then. The sand grows cold under my feet, and with Lucy lounging in the bay, there's nothing more for me out here.

"Can't say I've had the misfortune of reading it. Enjoy the beach. Don't get too close to the water. Not sure how Lucy feels about augmented humans, but meat is meat and I'm sure she won't mind picking wires out of her teeth."

Thames is standing along my path back to the compound. I'm hardly tired. There's been far too much excitement today for me to sleep without properly exercising some of the excess "energy" still bubbling in my core. I wonder if there are any soldiers brave enough to lie with a witch around.

As I pass him by, already plotting who I might play with for the evening, Donarick's hand catches my bare bicep.

"You didn't answer my question."

Coriander and cloves with a hint of cucumber... It's the oddest scent I have ever experienced, yet on this man it somehow works. Perhaps, it's the sea salt cutting into the freshness of the cucumber smell. Who knows?

"What question?"

"How does it feel to bring a country to its knees?"

I scoff.

"I'm far more interested in finding a half-decent looking man willing to go to his knees for me, but I doubt I'll find anything even resembling that in this cesspool of toxic masculinity."

"Too few men know how to properly worship a woman of your power."

"Guess I'll have to settle for a lackluster performance as usual."

I brush him off, but his other hand comes up, wrapping around my waist to grasp my other arm.

"I knew the moment I saw you that you would achieve great things, Miss Helsdottir."

The heat from his body melts into my skin, a sharp contrast to the cold metal of the ring on his finger.

"Sir?"

He isn't much taller than I am.

"Donarick. Call me Donarick, and I will be as a slave to your every desire."

Taken aback, I pivot to him, disbelief across my face.

"I mean it, Summer. You have cast an utmost powerful spell over me, and I can't find it in myself to wish it gone. So, I bid you, call me by my name, and I will do everything in my power to bring you unending happiness."

"Very well, Donarick. Prove it and turn off your augmentations."

If my demand stuns him, he doesn't show it.

He steps away and finishes unbuttoning the rest of his shirt. The fabric falls aside to reveal a lightly muscled torso. It would be hardly any different from any other man's chest I've seen were it not for the metal plate stitched into his left breast. A small monitor alights there: a little rectangle with a pulsing line through the center and spiking at the center with the rise and fall of his chest like a heart rate monitor. I can't be sure what kind of augmentation would require such an expensive decoration or what its use might be, but the scar tissue surrounding it is ugly. Crisscrossing striations and surgical scars from where staples and stitches once pulled the flesh together. He must catch my stare because he answers my unasked question.

"Before I was even born, one of my heart valves didn't develop properly. They cut me out of my mother's belly when I was three months premature, and I had my first heart surgery just four hours later. I can't even count how many operations I've had since. My father says I need to prove myself worthy of the doctors' efforts to save my life. Otherwise, all of their time, money, and talent would have been spent on a no account better off dead in his mother's womb. Naturally, my mother disagreed, not that her opinion meant much to him. The doctors advised her to abort me, and for her stubbornness, she gave her life. I think that's why my father hates me so much."

I don't know whether to apologize or laugh. The woman who gave birth to me—whether by choice or by law, I'll never know—left me on the side of the road still covered in birth fluids without even a name. I was the product of rape, you see, and I suspect the brute who fathered me was a hexen of some sort. A babe born unwanted and left to suffer the surname Helsdottir.

"This," he taps the plate on his chest, "is a daily reminder that were I not born into a human+ society, I would have been dead before my life even began."

"What happens if you turn it off?"

"What happens when a clock stops ticking?"

"So, you're telling me you'll die if you turn off your augmentations?"

"Not exactly. A clock doesn't die just because it stops ticking. There's just no guarantee it can be fixed after the fact."

"Meaning?"

"My chances of suffering a heart attack will rise by about 25% if I were to honor your request and power down my augmentations."

"Ah, so no turning off of augmentations then. Gotcha. I guess, I'll find my fun elsewhere—"

"I am telling you this not to deny you, Summer. I merely wish to be sure you understand the length to which I risk everything for you."

"You can't be serious. You might die."

He presses a button, and the ticking heart rate monitor turns black on his chest.

"I am deathly serious, Miss Helsdottir."

A smirk pulls at my lips. He is powerless before me, vulnerable and foolishly naive. How titillatingly fresh! I pull the man into a kiss. I want to drink the power from his body and leave him spent in the grass.

"Alright, my lord. Let us dance under the moonless sky until that heart of yours quits itself."

I fuck the human into the ground, and every time I worry that his body has had enough, he begs me for more.

Two days later, before I am scheduled to return to Seraphim with Donarick, Yggfret asks me a favor, and it deals with Wren fucking Nocturne.

I don't know why he wants me to force a draught of false death down some technomancer bitch's throat, but who am I to question a king?

CHAPTER 4 -

Canon in D minor

I thought I was the one in control. I thought I was the one with the power.

But then again ... every addict thinks they hold the reins until the cart flips over.

TWO MONTHS LATER - VATIDOME CITY - Thames' Residence

It happened at dinner.

I've been spending more and more time with Donarick. So much so that my fellow witches tease me for having moved into his quarters. I haven't moved into his quarters, but if I have a few books stacked on his shelves and a few outfits hanging in his closet, that is my own secret to keep.

"Miss Helsdottir, I finally have the honor of making your acquaintance."

The appearance of Donarick's father this far from his mansion in Vatidomus City is neigh unbelievable in and of itself. Even my lover, and yes, he is my lover, seems to have been caught by surprise. He reorganizes the kitchen staff, changes the menu, and arranges for his father's favorite tastes. Not that the man notices or expresses any iota of thanks for Donarick's efforts.

"The witch who brought down the Vulcan."

Grease shines on his chin from the strip of pork he is still chewing. For a man so supposedly pious, the Pontiflex is a glutton. Heaping plates of every course circling his placemat, he uses his fork the way some use a sword, hacking and scoring through his meat and vegetables like a medieval squire.

I smile and force myself to swallow a carrot even though the gravy clinging to the man's jowls has made me lose my appetite. "I'm afraid you give me too much credit, Your Grace."

General Llywellyn grunts, the distasteful bastard. He follows the Pontiflex around like a puppy. Even if I could reconcile his behavior in Deriva with vengeance, I'll never forget the kind of torment that man inflicted on the non-princess of the island country. I saw them bagging the corpse after the fact. Well, not the corpse, just the limp body of a woman afflicted with magical malady.

"Too much credit, indeed. If I'd known bringing a pet to battle would be all it took to bring down Tlanextli, I would have brought my parakeet ages ago."

"I hardly think your parakeet could have felled the Vulcan, Llywellyn," says Donarick to which his father hums in affirmation.

"Yes, Archibald, I'm sure if you had only known, Miss Helsdottir's efforts would have been entirely unnecessary, but alas, she's pulled through for us." Another piece of chicken is felled by the man's chompers, quickly followed by a forkful of salad. "Honestly, when Donarick presented the idea of working with witches, I was afraid I'd have to have him committed to the sanitorium at last. Too fanciful, he's always been."

Another strip of bacon goes into his mouth. Has he even swallowed the last bite yet?

"Witches... I mean really, who could ever hope to gain any sort of traction with heathens?" Llywellyn laughs as the pontiflex's continues his insults. "I mean really Yggfret is a conniving old bat, hardly worth any amount of trust, but I suppose witches are not unsimilar to their lycan pets. Give them a bone and they'll kiss your hand every day until you have no more need of them. But you..." The pontiflex points his fork at me. "You Miss Helsdottir, I have to hand it to you. If there were any hexen whore worth her salt, it's you, and I hear my Donnie-boy has had more than a few helpings off that plate."

"Father!" shouts Donarick, slamming his fist down on the table. My wine glass trembles at the force of the punch. The pontiflex startles, turning to his son with wide eyes.

"My son?"

His apparent shock doesn't stop him from taking another draught of wine, though.

"You may come into my home. You may drink my wine and sully my table. You may even insult me however you see fit, but you will not disrespect Miss Helsdottir in such a way."

"Don—"

"No!" Donarick's chair, flung backward by the violence with which he stood up, clatters against the ground. "Miss Helsdottir has proven herself an asset to our cause. It is through her efforts that Deriva was brought down, and I..."

Donarick looks at me, a strange expression on his face.

"You what, my son?"

Donarick turns back to his father, determination written across his brow.

"I believe she is my soulmate."

My stomach drops out of my belly, bounces off my pelvis, and lodges itself in my throat.

"Soulmate?" Llywellyn scoffs. "What sort of hexen nonsense has she been filling your head with?"

"It is not nonsense," Donarick declares. He circles around the table to stand beside my chair. "And she is not the source of my newfound knowledge. This truth I know in my heart. Summer Helsdottir." Donarick settles on the floor beside me, one knee raised and a jewelry box in his right hand. "The last few months have been a whirlwind, and I know this may seem premature, but in the wake of our rising victory and the change it will bring, I know there is no one else I would want by my side."

He unfolds the box's lid to reveal a beautiful diamond ring.

"Donarick?"

I'd forgotten he was a man of means. As the only child of the Pontiflex, he is the sole inheritor of an entire estate beyond my wildest dreams.

"Will you be my bride, Summer?"

Surely, this is a fairy tale. Surely, I've warped myself into an alternate dimension. How is this even possible? What do I even say? A witch and a cyborg?

You say, "Yes."

There it is again, the lust for power. I don't know if I love Donarick. I don't know if I'm truly even capable of love. Well, no. That's a lie. I've always loved power. Power is the only thing that has ever kept me safe in this wretched world. Maybe, the right person, someone who comes with a caboodle of inherited power, can help with that cause. Help me fall in love with something other than power.

"Yes." The word leaves my mouth before I can control it. "Yes, Donarick, I will marry you!"

Before I even realize that I've left my seat, Donarick is spinning me up and around in the air. I'm laughing. I don't think I've ever laughed like this before. It's... It's exhilarating.

"So, I will one day welcome a grandchild of mixed heritage," says the Pontiflex.

The spinning comes to a halt. Donarick places me back on my feet.

"We haven't exactly discussed that yet but—"

"Donarick, my boy, if you would have just let me finish, you would have heard me regale Miss Helsdottir with praises for her abilities. She should be lauded as a queen among the hexen."

"Yes, but Summer and I—"

"What an intriguing combination of genetic might!" the Pontiflex continues without so much as acknowledging his son. "Perhaps they'll be a true super soldier. Oh, how proud they will make me!"

He laughs. Donarick looks gob-smacked.

"Doubtful, your grace," responds Llywellyn.

"I don't doubt it," he declares. "We've already seen how magic can prove useful to science. Miss Helsdottir's might during the assault on Deriva proved extraordinary indeed. I'm sure any child she bears will grow to be the most wondrous of beings, indeed. Now imagine if that little sapling were to be my grandson."

I say nothing and can only blink stupidly at my food. Well, it's nice to know the Pontiflex sees me as a suitable mate for his sole heir, albeit in a creepy, pervy, continuing-the-family-line kind of way. The forkful of salad I force into my mouth tastes like mowed grass. And why should it taste any different? I am apparently breeding stock.

"Well, come. Let's drink. We have much planning to do."

That's how I came to marry an aristocrat. I, an orphan abandoned on the side of the road, married Donarick just a few short weeks later. The Pontiflex himself conducted our ceremony. Private and intimate featuring the attendance of a few notable Seraphim generals and King Yggfret alongside a few other members of the coven. Monsieur Géant coiled flowers around my horns while Xochtli sewed sigils of power and good fortune into my skirts.

Dressed in white and wreathed in lace, I've never felt more like a princess.

There is much fanfare. People talking of the unification between our two races. Of how this cements the alliance better than any contract. How Seraphim will be truly unstoppable with witches on their roster.

I care not for these things.

All I care about is the way Donarick looks at me as I walk to meet him at the altar, like I am a goddess and he a slave meant only to worship at my feet.

I thought I was the one in control.

I wasn't.

CHAPTER 5

Intermezzo

I understand now why Yggfret saved this woman's life all those years ago. She was a technomancer then, a puppet to the League and unknowing of her own potential. Even after she found her magic, the League thought they could control her, and I suppose for a time they did. I wrote her off when I heard she killed herself. Just another mad witch like myself.

I was wrong. I see that now.

Seraphim never should have messed with this woman.

A YEAR AND A HALF LATER - VATIDOMUS City

They're outside. I hear them.

Donarick pulls me by the hand down the long corridors of the Vatidome. Centuries worth of classical artwork, fine tapestries, curtains strung with golden tassels, it all flies by unseen and unimportant compared to everything happening now. Soldiers run past us. They look at us like we're mad, running the wrong way when it is they who run to their deaths.

"Lock the doors!"

"Do not let them in!"

"Protect the Pontiflex!"

A blast sounds from outside, and the painted glass of one of the windows implodes. Rainbows of glass rain on our heads, yet Donarick doesn't stall. While the guards turn to the onslaught of firepower, he angles us down the next passage and into one of the study halls. He lets go of my hand to slam the door shut and then promptly kicks a nearby desk into the wall.

"Dammit! It's all gone to hell thanks to that cursed witch."

I know who he's talking about: Wren Nocturne, back from the dead and toting along a host of magical might as never before seen. Well, it's difficult to come back from the dead when you never really went there to begin with. Yggfret, you damned fool! That draught of false death did its job, and the former technomancer returns for her vengeance. She already got Llywellyn. Donarick saw the aftermath of that attack and heaved. Now, the damned witch has snuck through our barrier, broken the circle maintaining it, and allowed her allies to make their way to the Pontiflex's throne room.

We've been winning up until now. Seraphim was winning all thanks to its alliance with some of the most powerful witches in Deus. Murasaki didn't know what hit them when ghouls invaded their mainframes. The Sekmetians didn't understand why their network was constantly experiencing interruptions. They certainly didn't realize their locators were being redirected to carefully constructed ambushes, and the Aighneans, they thought their equipment malfunctions were merely misfires, devastating explosions perfectly timed to occur the moment they aimed their canons at Seraphim's forces.

It was all us. The witches of Seraphim. Pulling the strings of battle without anyone ever even suspecting magic was in use.

Go figure, it would be a witch on the other side that brings it all tumbling down. We never did understand how the Alliance managed to reclaim Deriva. Now we know.

My ravens have been trying to keep her in sight but tracking a necromancer through a forest of death is nigh impossible. After the circle went down, I knew my fellow witches had fallen to the woman's deathly touch. I wasn't one of the witches maintaining the circle, but I was crucial to its success. My job was to hold a parameter around the coven to warn us of any oncoming danger. It's the setup we've been running for months now during every major battle. Today, we simply orchestrated it on a grander scale, trusting the technomancers to keep us safe while we kept them in a cozy little bubble of anti-tech wards. No one bothered to ask who would keep them safe from a witch on the opposite side. Why would they when no one knew she was there to begin with?

I stepped away from the circle when the signature of one of my ravens went dark. I found the poor thing pinned to a tree. His wings had been nailed to the top two corners of a triangle, the tail left to dangle down to the point. His beak was splayed open and his tongue ripped out. It was as I was pulling my raven from his dying place that a purple circle materialized on the ground. One of my compatriots fell through the reverse summon. It was Géant with a single-worded message.

"Run."

And in the next moment, he toppled over dead.

The giant witch tried to use my summoning circle in reverse. He must have wound up transporting himself through a dud plain of existence because his magical network was completely jacked up. I tried to revive him, but it was like sticking my hands in a mangled plate of leftover spaghetti.

Then, the barrier fell.

How did I know? I didn't. Not until a drone nearly blasted my head clean off.

By the time I got back to the circle chamber, they were gone. All of them. Every witch whom I had formed a bond with in the last two years, dead on the ground, and at the center, one raven-haired woman oozing necrotic power.

I did the only thing I could think of. I took Géant's advice. I ran.

Yggfret, the bastard, had to have known this would happen. He must have with his divine sight and fortune telling nonsense. And he allowed it all to happen. Hel! He designed it.

"She's destroyed everything!"

Donarick, my love, is frightened. I smell it in his sweat. I don't know when I became so attuned to my husband. My heart aches so badly for this man, I can barely breathe, but I suppose that's what all of us say when we fall in love with someone. And now...

"Killing Llywellyn, warning the Alliance of our pact with witches, wearing down our resources one outpost at a time, and now she's taken down your comrades. If only I'd realized sooner they had a witch on their side. Our last defense—"

Now the house of cards comes tumbling down, and we'll be going down with it. Or perhaps the more accurate way to put it would be coming down on our heads.

"Don, calm down. It isn't over yet. We can still win this."

"No, we can't. It's over, Summer. We don't have enough technomancers to stand up against the Alliance, and the coven... they're dead, and we will be soon to follow. It may not be today. It may not be tomorrow. But eventually the Alliance will arrange our execution for the whole world to see."

He's right. I know he's right. We've made our bed; now it's time to sleep in it. The coup is over; our forces fall one by one before our very eyes. I've never wanted to smash the surveillance monitors so much as a pair of adepts in Alliance colors shoot down the guards stationed at the front gate of the compound. Discovery at this point is unavoidable, and the fate that will follow after... I know how the League conducts their business. They've done it to hexen since the earliest days of the war.

The Pontiflex will be killed. Who will it be, I wonder, to strike down my dear father-in-law? There are any number of adepts thirsty to put an end to this war by any means necessary. As his last living child, my Donarick will be humiliated, ripped of his augmentations, and paraded before the masses as a lesson to those who would defy the League. Then, when they've had their last laugh, they'll stage his execution on a televised broadcast just as they once televised the executions of the last hexen aristocrats in their own throne rooms. It is a fate written as clearly in the stars as it will be on paper. Unless...

"What if the Alliance gains a new ally?"

"What?"

"You, my love. You will become the alliance's new ally."

Madness...

"I'm not following, Summer."

"We will declare you as an ally to the League. You will denounce the Pontiflex and save yourself from the damnation being his son will bring you."

Donarick wrings his sleeves between his fingers. It's a tick I've noticed he has in the face of tense situations. He did this after Xipilli's rescue. His father berated him badly, even struck him for losing such a vital hostage. I know because I was the one who had to mend his broken ribs later.

"You want me to betray my father?"

Traitor...

"It isn't betrayal if you were never on his side to begin with."

"What do you mean?"

"We aren't on your father's side, my love. We aren't on the League's side. We aren't even on the hexen side. We are on our side."

"That's a fine sentiment, darling, but I don't think they can distinguish Seraphim from us very easily, Summer. We've been too enlaced with this side of the warfront."

"Not if you broadcast yourself as a double agent."

"A spy?"

Oh, my poor innocent, Donarick.

"Yes, a spy. You can say you were acting as a spy."

"And how will we do that? It isn't like I just put my hands in the air and say I was rooting for the Alliance all along."

"Wren Nocturne, their precious hero, is alive because you made it so."

"But that's not true."

"Yes, it is. You gave her a draught of false death the night she was captured, and when Llywellyn thought her dead, you arranged to have her stowed away someplace safe. Someplace where she could heal and become the Alliance's ace."

"What are you saying?"

"I am saying what I am saying, and whether it is true or not, it is what you are going to tell them."

"Summer, did you—"

"Does it matter?" I interrupt his question before it can fully form.

I did. But that is a truth that I will never speak aloud, not even to my dearest husband. Donarick's face closes. I can't read his expression anymore.

"So, we tell them I saved Lady Nocturne's life because I had an inkling she would be the key to taking down Seraphim? That's asinine, and even if they did buy it, it won't be enough to acquit us of our guilt."

"Not alone, no."

"So?"

"So, you kill the Pontiflex."

"You want me to kill my own father?"

His voice is hollow.

"He's already dead, Don. Living off borrowed time."

"He's my father." It's a weak protest. One spoken out of obligation more than fortification.

"And he killed you the moment he marched against the other nations. Please, my love, this is the only way."

There is a long silence as Don contemplates my proposal, and slowly but surely, his expression blooms open once again.

"What would you have me do?"

Donarick, my dawn, always so eager to please.

Did you know that demons are just the gods and goddesses the Christians couldn't tame? The ones they liked became saints. Like Brigid for example. No one has an issue with fertility and harvest goddesses, especially ones who welcomed all to their hearth with warm bread and strong wine.

The others... Let's just say Beelzebub wasn't a fan of the whole forgiveness of sins thing. He thought it rather trite that someone could simply beg forgiveness and receive it only to rinse and repeat the process over and over and over again.

Seems like a legit loophole to me.

I would never ask forgiveness for any of my sins. I know I don't deserve it, so why do I wish, so desperately, for those green eyes to offer it?

I instructed my lover to stab his father in the back in plain sight of the Alliance's top brass, and he followed my plan to a T. Pontiflex Catalan died staring his enemy in the face while his own blood shoved a knife between his ribs. Now my love gets to sleep in his own bed while the rest of Seraphim's forces rot away in the very dungeons he pulled me from. I've been hiding out in the woods for three weeks. Since he outgrew human-sized abodes, I've kept Jormungandr tucked away in a cave in the mountains. This is where I've been hiding, and while the magical terrarium I've set up for the serpent is a cozy temperature, I'm tired of sleeping in a bedroll made of moss and leaves.

"It isn't safe for you here."

"Oh, pish-posh. No one saw me."

I damn well know that. Sneaking into the Alliance's victory compound to see Donarick was a downright stupid idea, yet here I am. I always did think love made a person dumber. But no one looks twice at the help. I've stolen one of the maid's uniforms for this venture into enemy territory. Servants are invisible no matter what class of person they serve.

"You are absolutely insane, you know that?"

The man pulls me to him with a violent need. Our mouths slam together in a drawn-out kiss that is more blood and teeth than lips. There's no need to rush. We are in his private quarters. No one is going to disturb us. No one will even know I was here.

"I've been officially named a technomancer," he says once we come up for air, our sweaty bodies lying side by side in bed. There is a strange quality to his voice, like he is speaking more to the ceiling than to me.

"A technomancer!"

"They have also named me Seraphim's Head of State," he continues.

"But Seraphim doesn't have a Head of State."

He grunts.

"They are reconstructing Seraphim into a pseudo-democracy after Aighneas and Sekhmeti, and they've decided I am the best fit to rule until such a time as elections can be held.

"Don, this is great!" I jump from the bed in excitement. Pacing about the room, I begin to ramble off my dream. "You'll have all the privileges of a world leader. You always hated the way your father ran the country, and you've always thought so highly of hexen. If it weren't for Llywellyn's foolishness and your father's greed, your plan to unite witches and technomancers in combat would have changed the entire world for the better. I can gather the few witches left, and you can sway other +ies to your cause. With you as our leader, we could make Seraphim a place where hexen can live without being hunted. A true unification of Hexen and Human+ state."

Donarick's silence draws me to a sudden pause. In all of my ranting and planning and celebrating, he hasn't said a word, hasn't so much as moved.

He doesn't seem happy. Not in the least.

"Honey..."

"They are going to use me as a figurehead, Summer."

"What—"

"Do you realize what that means? I'll be some puppet for them to control. They'll pull the strings, and I'll have no choice but to dance for them lest I want us to end up right back where we were when the Alliance tore down those barricades."

"Don—"

"This is what I killed my father for? A meaningless costume and a handler who will whip me into my place should I so much as voice an opinion."

He hides the fleshy parts of his face in his hands. All I can see is that ever-glowing mechanical eye. He only ever turns it off when we make love; at all other times it glows this constant red.

"Do technomancers get to choose the color of their equipment's light sources?"

His flesh eye looks at me, confusion in that pale blue gaze. He probably thinks I'm insane.

"You mean our cyber energy signatures?"

"Sure."

"No. The color we radiate is the optical translation of our inner workings. The Murasakans call it qi or ki. We just call it the magnetic synapsis."

"Cool." These human+, so desperate to differentiate themselves from us that they make up all this useless terminology. "So, your inner aura is red."

"It isn't an aura, Summer. That's a magic thing."

Sounds like the same shit to me.

"Do you know what it means to have a red energy signature?"

He frowns.

"Summer…" There is a growl in his voice, but I digress.

"Red is the color of leaders and royalty. It is the color of passion and intense base power. It roots you into the earth so that you can grow taller than those around you like a redwood in a forest of saplings."

"Summer, what are you getting at?"

"You are no puppet, Donarick J. Thames." I settle back on the bed next to his hip. "You were meant to rule."

"Tell that to the new council."

"We don't have to. We'll show them."

CHAPTER 6

Oh, Fortuna

Men are like knives, you see. You can handle a thousand of them and never suffer an injury, but if you lose sight of how dangerous they are for one moment, you'll end up sliced open with your heart, and maybe even your body, bloody on the pavement.

PLOTS AND SCHEMES... SCHEMES AND plots... Whatever is the difference? I certainly haven't a clue, but Donarick seems to have gained a knack for them since our secret promise to one another in the quiet of his rooms. I would tell you all about the series of events that led to my husband's rise to power, but that would take too long, and I've never been one to spoil a good mystery.

It takes me a while to learn who our enemies are. President Gewalt can be sided with, if only temporarily. She values power over anything else. Pharaoh Rameses falls into the role of Primarch like a snake curled into an egg. He is an inconvenience. His hatred for hexen, not to mention his megalomania, makes him a dangerous leader. I don't know why the technomancers saw fit to elect him to office, but money talks. It's Ebele and Deriva, united by the marriage of Prince Chike Naga to Princesa Atzi Moctezumo, that pose the real problem. Their young daughter represents a future unification beyond what is occurring even now. Goddess forbid the princesa's latest pregnancy results in a son. Then my Donarick will really be on the outs of a strong alliance. Not to mention the danger of that alliance growing a third leg with the ever-growing relationship between one Wren Nocturne, the heroine witch of Deriva, and Prince Kaito Miyazaki of Murasaki no Yama.

But worrisome romances are easily dealt with.

Suffice to say it was my idea to have the new primarch meet an untimely end, but it was my husband's brilliance that shooed a second bird out of our hair at the same exact moment. It was just too much to hope Wren Nocturne would stay gone.

"What do you mean you didn't manage to kill the target?"

To say my husband is displeased would be an understatement. Donarick is livid. It's been nearly a year since Rameses' murder, and we thought it high time to continue our push to bring greatness to Seraphim. However, his plot to kill a heavily pregnant princesa and her young daughter as a means to weaken our opposition has fallen through.

The being at the foot of my husband's threshold is no technomancer. It isn't even a cyborg by any such standard. It is something more, something off the grid that shouldn't exist, yet here it is not so much in the flesh as in the metal. Man-made and designed, it looks like any other machine I might find in the League: silver enameled with copper plates and few patches of skin to mimic humanity. There are wires and bolts and the smell of oil, but this is no ordinary bot. This robot is the stuff of even a technomancer's nightmares.

"The target wasn't alone," the android reports. "They had an escort with them."

"And who was this escort that a Freed One such as yourself couldn't manage to assassinate a pregnant princess and her screaming toddler?"

The sigil on its chest glows in even the bright light of the overheads. A Freed One: the technomancers may have made its body, but the witches gave it sentience. Now, neither the hexen nor the human+ wish to have anything to do with them.

"My database shows it was the half-sister."

Wren Nocturne... I can hardly believe it. This information comes to us after a long search for the woman who murdered Pharoah Rameses, or should I say Primarch Rameses? His removal from office paved the way for Gewalt to take over. Aighneas happily fills the role of superpower with their former president leading all of the League. The Technomancer Council has been on the hunt for Wren Nocturne ever since. A foot race between them and her dear brother who so desperately wants to find her before they do. They'll never find her, though, neither the new Vulcan nor the council. She's disappeared from the League's surveillance. It'll take a witch to find her, and there are so few of those left to call on, yet here she is protecting her half-sister from assassination.

"Wren Nocturne has been in hiding for almost an entire year. Why would she show up now?"

"The data is inconclusive, Mr. Thames."

"Then what good are you!" shouts Donarick. The robot tilts its head a quarter of an inch to the side. There is murder in that head tilt, and I don't think my husband realizes just how much.

"Perhaps she caught wind that her sister was in danger, my love."

Donarick shoots a sharp glance in my direction. I'm not supposed to draw attention to myself, but the robot doesn't care. In fact, the head tilt of death reduces ever so slightly. I raise my eyebrows at Donarick, offer my own head tilt, and silently tell him to get himself in fucking order. He blinks at me with his mechanical eye.

"My apologies, Freed One. You should have your credits delivered as arranged, minus the portion you would have received upon the success of your mission."

The robot makes a beeping sound as it checks the status of its account. "Yes, everything seems to be in order."

"Wonderful, now leave us," commands Donarick, and the mechanical assassin pivots to march out of the room. "I didn't realize failure could be so expensive—Argh!!"

Don's hands fly to his face. He curls in on himself in pain while his tech goes on the fritz. I rush to his side. The headaches are getting worse. Ever since his operation, he has been suffering from a constant influx of migraines and low-level seizures. The doctors said it would be normal to have such instances as his body gets used to the new tech configuration, and that the effects should wear off after a few months. It's been a year, and if anything, the symptoms are getting worse, but does he go to the doctor? No. He likes the power too much, and any chance of having the privileges of a tech-nomancer would be ripped away at a moment's notice if they found out he was suffering tech rejection. Because that is what this is—his body rejecting the augmentations.

"Don," I call, offering him a vial of potion from my breast pocket. He downs it before it even gets the chance to settle in his finger. It might seem like hyperbole to say the effect is instantaneous, but it really is. Donarick's brow relaxes and his shoulders ease as the pain dissipates.

Did you know that Basilisk tears have properties that can paralyze cell growth if ingested? Sounds like a perfect poison, I know, but for someone suffering implant rejection or cancer, it works better than chemo or radiation. It's the only thing that makes the symptoms disperse. Well, that and head scritches. He always likes it when I card my nails over his scalp. He basks in the attention for whole minutes before finally speaking again.

"All of our planning wasted…"

"Not wasted, my love. Just a minor setback."

"Perhaps, but how could she have known? Not even my people knew of our plans."

"I suppose it's possible she was simply visiting."

"An outlaw witch visiting her aristocratic sister. Preposterous!" A clatter sounds from the back of the hall. Donarick huffs. "You'd better have something worthwhile to share, Corax, because I am not in the mood for more bad news."

Out of the shadows behind Donarick's tapestry creeps a large rodent. The oversized muskrat is the size of a small dog and twice as cute, but once the creature makes its way out of the corner, it shifts. Muscles lengthen, fur disappears, teeth shorten, and high-pitched squeaks become deep groans until a naked man stands at the center of the room. A ruffian lycan if I've ever seen one, there's nothing ratty about his human shape. More than six feet tall with a mane of thick brown hair, Corax's oversized husk dwarfs even the former Pontiflex's throne.

"I might have the answer to your question, my liege."

"Corax," sighs Donarick. "You know how much disdain I have for your habit of eavesdropping."

"You don't seem to have any problem with it when I am gathering information for you."

"Touché."

"My sources state that Lady Nocturne was visiting the princesa about some increasingly personal matters."

"What personal matters?" I ask.

"There are rumors, my lady. Rumors the witch is keeping a child with her in the forest."

"A child?"

"Yes. A young girl. Can't be more than three years old."

Donarick laces his fingers together in contemplation.

"A wartime babe. How interesting?"

I don't like the way he says that. It's too keen.

"Is it hers?" I ask. A part of me hopes it isn't. Surely, it can't be. I wasn't exactly there to watch when the woman broke her brother out of Llywellyn's makeshift prison in Deriva, but I know what happened, how she essentially sacrificed herself and her freedom for her brother, and everyone knows what happens to women who become prisoners of war. Yggfret said she was almost truly dead by the time he dropped off her body at the hospital.

"There can be no way of knowing," answers Corax. "The number of war orphans roaming the continent... she could have just picked up a stray. She frequents an orphanage in Lorelei, bringing gifts of food and money."

"Perhaps, she adopted a street urchin," I add.

"Doubtful," mewls the lycan. "A woman like that taking in a stray. Ha! She can barely take care of herself. Why would she take care of someone else's brat?"

The lycan has a point. Not that I've ever thought much of the intelligence of lycans, but if it is hers, that would mean the child was conceived right at the beginning of the war when... My stomach tightens. That is a fate I would wish on no one, not even my worst enemy.

"I don't believe it." No woman should have to carry a fetus she doesn't want, much less one put there by an enemy. "It isn't possible." Surely, she would have gotten rid of it as quickly as she could.

But what if she didn't get the chance?

"There is a way to find out," whispers Donarick, a calculating look in his eye.

"Don?"

My love's eyes are alight with inspiration. A lightbulb has gone off in his head and his new optical augmentation shines ever brighter for it. My spine straightens and I hold my chin just a little higher. This is the man I married. This is a man who deserves to be king, not some no-account-brat born into royalty like the new Miyazaki Emperor or Moctezumo Vulcan.

"Can you imagine the potential, Summer? A child born of a technomancer and a witch. A super soldier indeed."

"But it's a child, my love."

"Children grow up."

"Yes, but…"

He doesn't seem to hear me. The noise of his own plots is far too loud. It's kind of sexy seeing him like this even if whatever seems to be brewing in that mind might be bitter to drink. This is the man I would follow to the ends of Deus. Donarick J. Thames, my savior who kept me from another technomancer's torment on one dark and lonely night while I sat waiting in a cold, barren cell.

"Darling, I have a new mission for you."

This kind of arousal, terrible and terrifying, shouldn't be possible.

"Of course, my love." He knows I'll do anything for him. "Whatever you would have me do, so long as you think me suitable for it."

"My beautiful Summer, you know I have full faith in you."

I can't help but smile into the kiss. After all, I've never failed him before.

CHAPTER 7

Melancholia

Once upon a time, there was a fair maiden who loved a
handsome knight.

One day, while the maiden was traveling, she found, in her
pocket, a secret gift.

But she was on a dire mission, one which could crumble nations.

And so, the gift was kept secret and safe inside her pocket.

This gift, she cherished and kept to herself to return to her
handsome love.

But when the time came to open the present, all she found was a
meek dead dove.

I AM FIRST CLUED INTO MY CONDITION WHEN a lycan comes up and sniffs my pelvis. I know, rude! The creature has the audacity to look at me like I assaulted her when I punch the beast away with a blast of magic designed to force her out of her wolfish skin.

"I didn't mean you no harm, witchy."

"Yeah, well keep your nose to yourself."

I had every right to sock the wolf in the nose and am about to do so again when her eyes go canine, and she sniffs the air again.

"I ain't never met a pregnant witch before. Smells down-right deeeelicious."

The she-wolf licks her chops, and I let loose my spell. Dark electricity zings from my fingertips into the lycan's body, and before the beast can properly reorient itself, I summon a steed and hurry away.

I suppose I should have known it was a possibility that I might get pregnant way back when we started this whole affair—the birds and the bees are an inescapable matter of course, after all—so I do the responsible thing and take a test. Ornery things, pregnancy tests. It takes me nearly four days to find a halfway decent one. I'm not exactly in sophisticated territory. The hexen centers between Seraphim and my destination are controlled by vampyres and lycans, neither of which have much need for pregnancy tests. Lycans reproduce so rapidly, it's easier for one to already be pregnant than not, and vampyres can't get pregnant, which leaves only a small populations of unaugmented humans, witches, and various asunder hexen demanding the pee-sticks, and the ones here are some diabolical mix of two unbelievably archaic methods of pregnancy prediction: injecting pee into a frog and watering a patch of barley with it. Not a fan.

By the time I finally find some counterfeit tests made to mimic the ones in the League, I am well beyond late for my cycle.

I don't know how the humans have the patience for them. Too many steps and the involvement of bodily fluids and then you have to set a timer, and after the little line turns blue, you then need to press the button to do a self-guided ultrasound. I mean, I suppose it's cool and convenient for people who are used to that kind of thing, but the ultrasound stick makes me itch at the thought of using it, yet here I am prodding my gel-slick belly with it. I'll admit it's pretty neat seeing my little witchling in the holograph. An aura reading spell would have been much easier to do, but the pregnancy test was able to tell me how far along I was: 12 weeks—just long enough for a little bundle of cells to pulse with a sure-fire strength in that tiny projection even if the creature pictured looked more like one of my summons than anything remotely human.

When I perform an aura reading, I can tell it will be a boy, and my skin warms with happiness. The knowledge of my future offspring.

Shhhh...
Hush little baby, don't you cry.
Mama's gonna buy you an alibi.
And if that alibi falls flat,
Mama's hands are stained red beyond a fact.

The young prince is born on the 4th day in the Month of Light. A very auspicious day, if the stars are to be believed, but the child has been born under a false sign, for while the new parents know it not, their son is not long for this world. Not if I have anything to do with it.

They once called me the baby thief.

Baba Yaga would have been proud of my accomplishments back then, but I am not proud of that time. I do not take pride in causing harm to the innocent, but every witch knows the best results stem from the worst of deeds.

It isn't difficult stealing a baby. So many parents are taught the importance of separate sleeping arrangements. Put the baby in another room, make the baby sleep in a bassinet, and if the mother is of royal blood, have a wet nurse come in to feed the child.

I steal into the palace riding on the wings of an invisibility spell and a distraction made by some of my more virulent summons. The gremlins may not be from this area of the world, but they cause plenty of mischief. It's always fun to see how the human+ deal with their technology being turned topsy turvy.

This late at night, I was expecting him to be asleep. He is paler than his parents, but I can see the dark caramel tones of his mother's exotic complexion beneath that creamy, newborn skin. In fact, just looking at the babe, he seems to have more of his mother in him than anything else. Is there a chance he isn't really the heir to the throne? No. He has his father's eyes. The prince's child looks at me with dark chocolate eyes.

The poor little thing has no idea who I am, yet his lips quirk up into a gummy grin as I peek over the edge of his crib. It's probably just gas. I know that somewhere in my mind, yet it's still strangely endearing.

I'm supposed to kill this child. That is my mission: to kill the Naga heir, so that Seraphim will not lose power.

I'm supposed to kill this child?

I know I'm supposed to. It's for the greater good of all of us, but for some reason, I hesitate.

The babe cries. Loud, piercing wails that will summon my trackers straight to me if I don't keep pace, and I don't know if I can keep this flight up. My insides are burning and it's hard to draw a breath.

Jormungandr carries me as well as he can, but he is no Kukulkan or Quetzalcoatl. Those serpents were born of the sky. Basilisks, on the other hand, are born of the earth. They can't fly, and there is only some much a ground escape can do against an aerial pursuit.

"Ahh!"

A drone swoops overhead. Sharp steel claws grasp for my head and hair, but I duck away, bending forward over the wriggling bundle in my arms. The metal rips straight through my jacket and opens my shoulder all the way to the bone.

The infant cries harder, and another pang flexes through my abdomen. Is Gideon kicking? He's never struck me so hard before.

"Cease all lethal measures!" a staticky voice over the radio cries. "The witch has our newborn prince hostage. Do not take any action which might injure the baby."

"*Knuse!*" I shout, thrusting my wand in the direction of the drone. Void magic furls around its body. A moment later, the drone breaks apart into particles. All the microscopic bits of ions and protons that make the machine a physical thing disperse into much simpler, less dangerous pieces. Perfect packaging for sending something to another dimension where particles can't form bonds.

My lip quirks up in a half smile. Even the baby in my arms seems to celebrate my success, having quieted in the wake of my spell. My belly, just barely starting to round at my 23rd week of pregnancy, becomes uncomfortably tight.

My knees clench together. Jormungandr swerves sideways as another drone shoots instead for the snake's seeing head.

Jormy's heads, unable to decide in which direction to evade the blast, split only to rebound into one another. If snakes could trip, this would be exactly what the netherbeast does. We tumble down the slope to land in the nearby ravine. The result is a tangled mess of serpent. At least, the dumb beast had the forethought to wind its scaly body around me and my charge. Otherwise, we would have been thrown goddess-knows how far away.

"Over here! I've got her in my scopes."

Faen! They've found me. I can hear them already scrambling down the ravine's edge.

"I hear the baby. He's alright."

"Is the witch dead?"

"No idea."

Not dead. Not dead at all, and that will not be changing anytime soon. Holding the baby in one arm, I dip my fingers in the open wound on my shoulder. Through clenched teeth, I grit out the words of the spell while drawing a reverse-summoning circle in my own life blood.

"Lous eht os, esrevinu eht sa, tuohtiw, nihtiw sa, woleb os, evoba sa."

The circle glows with anti-light. Magic falls from my being into the earth. It's like being pulled from a bucket of water fully clothed. The weight seeps into my limbs, into my core, into my heart. I am sinking into my circle. When I am knee deep in the space-time riff, pain buckles in my core, doubling me over.

What the—! Gideon?

Reverse summoning is dangerous on even the unburdened body. What will it do to an unborn?

I hesitate. My body lightens and the circle pushes me out. With the few inches that I rise, I must enter the adepts' field of vision because no sooner do I unbreech than the lasers rain down.

"No!" I duck down, screaming. Apparently, these adepts have a different interpretation of what it means not to "injure the baby." "*Esrevinu eht sa...*"

The portal draws me back down. Jormungandr's scales disappear inch by inch into the void's dry waters.

"*Tuohtiw, nihtiw sa, woleb os—!*"

Another pain right in the basin of my pelvis.

"*Evoba sa!*"

My voice sounds like a rampant animal. I don't even recognize it. The pitch is wrong. There is a roaring quality to it layered over a volatile hiss like one of the old things I make a point to avoid by summoning creatures out of the deep between dimensions.

I'll be traveling right alongside them tonight.

My body, already heavier with my growing babe, drops down into the pit, and the infant screams along with me.

Where I land, the light is dim. It is just before dawn in this part of the world. I recognize the place. It's my Jormungandr's usual cave, lined with moss and decorated with heat orbs for my darling reptile. It is a place that is normally dry and warm, yet I am cold and wet.

Water has soaked through my pants, tremors run up and down my spine, and a deep rolling pain comes and goes in the pit of my belly. Underneath me, a pool of blood begins to form.

No... It's too soon. It's way too soon. And there is no one here to help me.

When it's all said and done, I lay spent and exhausted.

To my right, one bundle of linens wriggles and cries, hungry and tired from the trauma they have just endured. To my left, another bundle of linens lies still, the babe within blue and battered from the ordeal it didn't have the strength to survive. My heart, a broken thing in my chest, bleeds at a life that never really had a chance to live fades from this world. The surviving infant writhes, his screams for food reaching a fever pitch.

He looks so little like his father...
It's because he's mine.
He's mine. He'll always be mine.

Gideon is everything I could ask for. A happy babe who giggles when he sees me and gives the cutest burps every time he finishes his bottle. It was hard going at first. He didn't want the formula—not that I blame him really. Who wants to drink a disgusting concoction of cow's milk and synthetic breast milk enzymes? But he couldn't have my breast. I was afraid I was going to lose him, too, but eventually he began accepting the bottle, and we've settled into a routine ever since.

Sore from my delivery and weak from blood loss, I haven't yet garnered the energy to return home. I still haven't introduced him to Donarick. Soon. Very soon he will meet his father. Once it's safe. Once no one is looking anymore.

Jormungandr won't stay near me. I suspect it has to do with the smell of postpartum. I can barely stand the stench myself whenever I change my pad. Gideon is sleeping in his bassinet, a cushioned rock basin I've dug out, so I have somewhere to put him while he sleeps. Next to him, I keep unsullied diapers, bottles, and a cauldron I haven't checked the contents of in days.

I am cleansing my hands of my latest mission assignment when the footsteps find me.

"Summer."

"Who's there?"

I don't know this technomancer.

"I've been looking everywhere for you."

"You're not welcome here."

Inhuman eyes trail to the infant still swaddled in his basin.

"That isn't your baby."

"Yes, he is."

"No, he isn't, Summer, and I am taking him."

"No! He's my son. You won't take him away from me."

I lunge for my baby, but the technomancer's hand slaps me away. My head snaps to the side, my shoulders and hips follow, and my head hits the wall.

By the time I come to, my Giddeon is gone, and Donarick's sad human eye stares down at my prone form.

"My love, what did they do to you?"

"They took him. They took our son."

"Our son?"

"Gideon."

"We had a son…" Donarick looks from me to the bassinet and back, disbelief across his face. "Why didn't you tell me?"

"I'm so sorry, Don—"

He shakes me by the shoulders.

"How could you not tell me you were pregnant? What did you do with him?"

"They took him!"

"Who took him?"

"I don't know."

"You don't know." His fingers bruise into my shoulders. He shakes me again. My barely healed wounds from labor tear open. I gasp in pain. "You don't know!!"

"Donarick, you're hurting me."

He stops immediately.

"I'm sorry," he whispers. He lets go of my shoulders and threads his hands through my hair. "I'm sorry. I'm sorry. I'm sorry."

He mutters apologies into my temple, each word decorated with a sweet kiss. The light outside the basilisk's cave changes and then changes again until finally, Donarick's apologies cease. An eerie silence replaces them before…

"We will get him back."

CHAPTER 8

Staccato

Donarick was my rock after Gideon. He picked me back up, put me back together, and sent me off on my revenge.

He snaps the collar round my neck.

Ding Dong! The witch is dead. Which old witch? The wicked witch.

Ding Dong! The wicked witch is dead.

I'm dead...

One Month Later

WREN NOCTURNE IS DEAD. BY THE gods! Wren Nortune is dead but so is her young charge.

"I told you to get there first!"

It stings. The slap to my face stings. It wasn't a hard hit. Not really. Not compared to the second.

"I trusted you!"

The second strike knocks me off balance. My side collides with the banister. All this because I failed.

"I've kept you safe this whole time and this is how you repay me."

The man's chest heaves with exertion and rage. I've never seen him like this before, this unhinged, this heated, this out of control.

"Donarick," I start.

"Quiet!" The second hit is much harder. "The girl is lost because of you! Because someone beat you to the witch's hideaway."

"I did get there first. There was no one there, Don. Not a trace of a life to be found. The bombs, they—"

"Liar! You've mucked this all up, Summer. How could I have entrusted such an important task to a *hexen*!"

He spits the word out like a curse.

"But I—"

"Shut up!"

His ring cuts open my cheekbone. Blood wells at the site.

"Donarick, please. Your heart."

"Is none of your concern, witch!"

Another strike sends me rolling sideways, and the floor ends.

I've never fallen down stairs before. Never even imagined what it might be like. It happens in slow motion. First the ceiling waves at you then the carpet burns you. Painful, yes. Bruising, sure. Concussion, certainly possible. But that's only how they portray it on television or theater when the damsels hit the bottom with one shoe missing and their hair out of place only for prince charming to sweep them up and marry them.

That's not real life.

I never imagined there would be the crunching of bone, the snapping of tendons, or the head splitting agony of your skull opening.

The landing finds me like a bag of skin and pain. I can't move. I can't talk. I can't even open my eyes. And when a foot puts pressure on my head, darkness edges in.

I don't know what hurts worse, my broken body or my broken heart.

It's cold inside of my summoning circles. Void magic, while not as chilly as ice, is as bleak as the empty spaces between little known and unknown planes. I am a void magic user. It's my natural magic, gifted to me by the cursed genes that make me a witch. It's perfect for summoning creatures from said void. There's something comforting about dealing with "monsters."

Monsters are honest. Those elder things that lurk in space between the hands of time are the most honest beings I've ever come into contact with. They are living, breathing amalgamations of baser emotion: delight/delirium, desire/despair, destruction/death, dreams and deconstructions. These are creatures who drink madness. They consume it, let it curdle in their gut, and then spew it out into the nearest vessel for re-consumption. I've eaten their aforementioned puke, and they never lied to me about what it was. I did it willingly to gain their trust.

So, yes, it's dangerous, creeping into the in-between, but at least the creatures that reside there are truthful. Here on Deus, in reality, people will lie in your face, knock you down, and leave you there to stew in your own waste. But monsters... monsters will keep you warm if you just give them what they want, but the process of getting them here is like dropping yourself into a tub of ice.

It's cold in the circle. I hate the cold.

I suppose the one thing my mother did right by me was give me the name "Summer." Summer like the sun. Summer like a blissful vacation to the seaside. Summer like the heat that melts the edges off the pavement. But the cold... Not only is it uncomfortable, not only does it require preparation and survival skills, but it's also a thief. Cold usually comes with darkness. It invades from the deep places of the world to suck the heat from the ground. The cold will grip you by the throat and squeeze the life out of you. Collect your life-force for itself until there is nothing left for it to syphon off. Cold is for dead things, ice for the decaying, and frost is for the unmoving skin of the lifeless.

I am not a dead thing.

They say that witches who steal from their kin are damned... Is this my damnation?

Beep... buh-beep... beep... buh-beep...
There's cotton between my ears.

"Ah, you're awake. What a relief! We were afraid it would be weeks before you woke up."

Weeks? What happened?

"Where am I?"

"My name is Dr. Faust, and you are presently being treated at St. Brigid's Hospital."

"How did I get here?"

"Mr. Thames brought you in of course. Your husband was scared out of his wits when you fell down the stairs."

Is that what he told the doctors? That I fell down the stairs. What a convenient excuse... I suppose it isn't a lie. I did fall down the stairs.

"And where is my husband, now?"

"Anxiously awaiting your recovery. You've been in a coma for nearly 20 hours now."

A coma... The asshole put me in a coma!

"Well, your vitals are holding strong despite the dehydration. You were probably experiencing a bit of vertigo, which is why you fell in the first place. You've got a bit of bruising and swelling, but that is to be expected for someone who's just fallen down a flight of stairs. Thankfully, there's no injury to the baby."

The world grinds to a halt.

"What?"

"The baby is perfectly healthy."

"What baby?"

"Oh, I suppose congratulations in order. You're about eleven weeks pregnant. That's why we needed an ultrasound. Your urine analysis showed a presence of hCG, so we had to make sure the fetus was still viable after such a nasty fall. The good news is your little one's heartbeat is strong, and everything seems to be progressing as normal."

"Oh..."

"Yes, well, I'm sure your husband will be happy to hear the news. I can let him know when he comes back if you'd like."

"No," the answer comes all too quickly. "I-I'll tell him."

"As you wish. My nurse will be back with your discharge papers. Remember lots of fluids and don't forget to take your medications. I've prescribed you an antibiotic and a pain killer that should be safe for pregnancy. I recommend a follow-up as soon as possible with your OB. The first step to a healthy baby is good prenatal care. Which, by the way, you should get on a vitamin regiment asap."

"Right..."

The doctor turns his back on me as he walks out of the room. In my head, I am counting backward from my last period. I could've sworn I had one just two weeks ago, or was that something else, but the last time I bought a pack of tampons was over three months ago, and I bleed through a whole box every time. It can't have been that long. Could it?

Disbelief. That's what this is. Bone-deep disbelief... If only I could say it was helping with the pain. My ribs ache from the fall.

I've never wanted children. Not until my Gideon. I suppose I had him for a while, but... Why would I want to submit another life to this wretched world? And Donarick... There's a bandage on my cheek where his ring cut me and gauze wrapping my torso. It is only by fortune his treatment of my person didn't already cause a miscarriage.

Do I really want a life like this for a child?

CHAPTER 9

Lamentation

Did you know that in the old-world women of limited means used to purposefully roll onto their infants in the night to smother them to death? It was during a time that abortions were the worst sin a woman could commit. They made the mistake of confessing their crimes to Catholic priests who, as a result, deemed that any woman caught sleeping in the same bed as their babies would be excommunicated. 'Cause we can't have women of low status offering their babies a swift, painless, merciful death when the better option is that they starve their way into the afterlife.

The irony of it is that babies are far more likely to die in their sleep when made to sleep away from their mothers. Just look at the spike in SIDS rates in the Victorian Era when lacey nursery cribs were all the rage.

ABORTION IS ILLEGAL IN SERAPHIM, SO I travel all the way to Murasaki no Yama to get the treatments that I need.

The clinic I visit is clean. The workers there are warm if not friendly. They seem to understand that these kinds of decisions are not made lightly and that it's none of their fucking business why their patients choose the way they do. I use my husband's credentials, stolen without his knowledge, and receive VIP treatment.

I'm surprised by how painless the process is.

Were I to have undertaken the task at home, it would have involved ingesting goddess-knows how many toxins, and if that didn't work, well, the hanger-method is as dangerous as it is painful, but it is effective. There are magics that could be performed. Dark magics. Magics that involve sacrificial rights and surgical accouterments to even work. Magic capable of transferring a pregnancy from one woman to another, but that requires another participant willing to both experience pregnancy and work with a witch to do it (one of those might be easy to find... The other, well, I'm in hiding for a reason.), and my sadism stops at the idea of forcing someone to carry a pregnancy they don't want. Blood, yes. Murder, yes. Dismemberment, absolutely. But rape, no! And forced pregnancy... Absolutely not! Thor! Even witches have morals.

This early in the process, all I have to do is swallow a couple of pills and my body will expel the fetus naturally. If I'd waited any longer, I would have needed a D&C, but then they would have just put me under anesthesia and taken care of the business while I slept.

The nurse who brought me the medication gives me a tender smile as she tosses the pill case into the nearby bin.

"Alright, you're all done. You can get yourself dressed again."

As I redress, there is a niggling voice in the back of my head that keeps saying, "What if..." What if I kept the baby? What if I ran away and raised my child alone? What if I lived in a fairy tale world where hexen and human+ could live as one?

Tch, stop dreaming, Summer...

There's a small rustling sound from the bag I've set down on the exam table. The bag shifts, startling the nurse.

"Ma'am, I think there's something in your backpack."

"It's nothing," I say, grabbing the bag and tossing it over my shoulder. Something clatters around inside, but I pay it no heed and hurry out of the room. Once out onto the street, I duck into the nearest back alley to hide behind a dumpster. The fetid odor of the trash makes me want to gag, or maybe it's the early effects of the medicine. They did tell me nausea was a fairly common symptom. Summoned monsters! I didn't even think of that. How am I going to get home if I can barely keep my guts down?

The journey here has been long and taxing, not to mention filled with technomancers. The only way to enter Murasaki no Yama from Seraphim is via air passage or light rail, both incredibly risky and exceedingly dangerous for someone like me. So, I opted for another method of travel.

"You stupid animal," I curse, ripping the bag open. Inside a pair of slitted amber eyes stare back at me, framed in angry whiskers and an enchanted muzzle. Silje hisses at me from the confines of the makeshift prison I've stuffed her in. "You could have gotten us both caught and thrown out."

Another hiss for my troubles.

I don't even grace the feline with a response; I just stick my hand in the bag, wrap my palm around the cat's throat and, through gritted teeth, pull the power I want from her directly into my synapsis.

The yowling that ushers forth from the netherbeast's throat will echo in my dreams tonight. I just know it.

I wasn't always like this, you know. I wasn't always the kind of witch who would steal another's prized accoutrements. Stealing another witch's familiar... it's like stealing a piece of their soul, yet here I am torturing this one because it's the only displacer beast on this plane of existence and my only means of getting back to the manor before Donarick realizes I'm gone.

I toss the netherbeast back into her holding pen when I arrive home just minutes before Donarick returns from his trip to congratulate the newest technomancer initiates at their graduation ceremony in Aighneas. He's in a good mood. Three of Seraphim's adepts have passed the trials, making our roster of technomancers all the stronger.

Over the course of the next week, I suffer the worst cramps and the worst bleeding I have ever experienced in my life. There's something dark and sickly about miscarriage blood, even an intentional one. It's different from my normal cycle. There is no prospect of something new taking its place as my menstrua would normally be. No, this blood is purely destructive.

They say that women who have an abortion are forever damned in the eyes of the divine. They say we will be cursed to infertility and suffering for all the rest of our non-child-bearing years. They say... well, they say a lot of things that don't really matter at the end of the day. My abortionist wouldn't agree. I only met her once, but she was a lot kinder than some midwives I've met.

There was a midwife at the orphanage who would come only when called, and oh, how I hated her, the bitter old crone. Every so often, a woman would come, heavy with child and of no means to care for her burden. Some came wanting to give their children away. Others came asking for the help they would need to care for their child themselves. But regardless of their circumstance, all of them first needed to deliver their babies. So naturally, the midwife would have to deliver her baby, and my goddess, how she bullied those women. She shamed them for getting pregnant regardless of their circumstance. She let them labor for days only to cut them open when such a call should have been made much earlier. And no sooner would these babies be pulled from their hosts' wombs than they would be whisked off into the arms of their new parents. No concern for mummy dearest. Not even for the mothers who wanted to keep their babies. They were too young, too poor, too irresponsible. How could we allow them to raise a child?

That's how the orphanage would make its money, you see. FOR SALE: INFANT FRESH FROM THE WOMB

Because that's how prospective parents want their children, new and unsullied. A multi-million credit black market on babies, and no one so much as batted an eye.

Donarick is as sweet as ever. He thinks I'm just having a very bad period. He wipes the sweat off my forehead, brings me my favorite chocolates, and at the end of the week when the pain has dimmed and the bleeding slowed, he takes me out on the town to my favorite restaurant and a movie, and on the way home, he makes his proposal.

"I am tired of hiding you in the shadows, my love."

"Don," I whisper. "I know it isn't safe for me—"

"I've devised a plan to bring you into the open as my true wife and soulmate."

He takes my hands in his own, and for a moment I am seeing the man who asked me to marry him in deference to his own father insulting me from across the table. It's almost as if the last four years haven't even happened. Like I haven't just flushed our baby down the toilet because I couldn't trust him to treat them like a human being rather than a lab rat.

"What do you mean?"

"Chiamaka."

Not what I was expecting.

"What about Chiamaka?"

Since the untimely death of her father and brother, Chiamaka has proven herself a fiercely protective lioness not only of her young, orphaned niece but also of her country, taking the reins until her young charge reaches the age of majority.

"She is the one we need."

"She'll never come around. Not so long as her niece draws breath."

"Who needs a willing partner when I have a willing witch?"

I raise my eyebrow.

"What does that have to do with anything?"

"My darling, are you familiar with a type of magic called a glamour?"

I wish I could say I was stabbed in the back. It would be easier that way. But I can't. My death came from right beside me.
I guess you could say I was blindsided.

Summer may no longer be of the living realm, but her touch is far from gone. Will she find her own justice in Wren Nocturne, the witch she hated so much?

The only way to find out is to join us in the next installment of The Nocturne Symphony: Scherzo.

Fine

AFTERWORD

Domestic abuse is a horrible reality of our world. If you or someone you know has suffered in an abusive relationship, silence is never the answer. Remember, we are all fighting our own battles, some more haunting than others. Kindness is always a choice.

Below is a list of help services for survivors of domestic abuse:

- The National Domestic Violence Hotline
  1-800-799-7233 (SAFE)
  www.ndvh.org
- National Dating Abuse Helpline
  1-866-331-9474
  www.loveisrespect.org
- National Child Abuse Hotline/Childhelp
  1-800-4-A-CHILD (1-800-422-4453)
  www.childhelp.org
- National Sexual Assault Hotline
  1-800-656-4673 (HOPE)
  www.rainn.org
- National Suicide Prevention Lifeline
  1-800-273-8255 (TALK)
  www.suicidepreventionlifeline.org

- National Center for Victims of Crime
  1-202-467-8700
  www.victimsofcrime.org
- National Human Trafficking Resource Center/
  Polaris Project
  Call: 1-888-373-7888 | Text: HELP to BeFree (233733)
  www.polarisproject.org
- National Network for Immigrant and Refugee Rights
  1-510-465-1984
  www.nnirr.org
- National Coalition for the Homeless
  1-202-737-6444
  www.nationalhomeless.org
- National Resource Center on Domestic Violence
  1-800-537-2238
  www.nrcdv.org and www.vawnet.org
- Futures Without Violence: The National Health
  Resource Center on Domestic Violence
  1-888-792-2873
  www.futureswithoutviolence.org
- National Center on Domestic Violence, Trauma &
  Mental Health
  1-312-726-7020 ext. 2011
  www.nationalcenterdvtraumamh.org

INDEX

Glossary of Characters

By Appearance

Summer Helsdottir (Hexen) – Summing Witch. Married to Donarick Thames in secret.

Montwyatte (Technomancer) – Archibald's right-hand man. A cyborgean brute known for his hostility and aggression.

Donarick J. Thames (Adept) – Son of Pontiflex Catalan. Enters into a whirlwind romance with Summer Helsdottir.

Yggfret Bloodfang (Hexen) – The Goblin King. A powerful witch and leader of the Hexen who join Seraphim's forces during the war.

Monsieur Géant (Hexen) – A half-giant witch boasting superhuman strength.

Xochtli (Hexen) – The bruja of the Mojavan Desert.

Howard P. Thames – Pontiflex Catalan of Seraphim – Religious leader of Seraphim and father to Donarick Thames.

Archibald Llywelyn – General of Seraphim – Father of Oswald Llywelyn.

Atzi Moctezumo – Princess of Deriva – Eldest daughter of Tlanextli and wife of Chike Nagi. Mother of Zenza Nagi.

Wren Nocturne – The youngest child of Tlanextli Moctezumo – 247th Trials Graduate – Known Alias: The Songstress of Lorelei.

Chike Nagi – Crown Prince of Ebele – 247th Trials Graduate – Husband of Atzi Moctezumo and Father to Zenza Nagi.

Chiamaka Nagi – Princess of Ebele – Younger sister to Chike Nagi and Zenza's paternal aunt.

Rameses Sahra – Pharaoh of Sekhmeti – Father of Jamar Sahra. First Primarch of The League.

Morrigan "The Morrigan" Gewalt – President of Aighneas. Elected Primarch after the death of Rameses.

Book Club Questions

1. How does Summer change over the course of the story?

2. Would you consider Summer to be a reliable narrator? Why or why not?

3. What event caused the biggest shift in Summer's persona?

4. What do you think might be happening behind the scenes to influence Donarick's treatment of Summer?

5. Why does Summer stay?

6. What is Summer's motivation throughout the story? Does it change? Why?

7. Which aspects of the story do you think were derived from mythology? How does your knowledge of mythology affect your perception of the creatures featured in the story?

8. Do you think Summer should have handled her pregnancies differently? Why or why not?

9. How do her experiences mirror that of real women around the world?

10. If you were in her situation, would you have made a similar or different choice?

11. What are a few of the more Lovecraftian elements of the story? How does this affect your perception of Summer?

12. What are your personal thoughts about Summer? Is she a redeemable character?

13. At what point in the story do you think Summer reached her point of no return? When was her ultimate fate sealed?

14. In the series proper, Summer can be arguably seen as a foil for Wren Nocturne? How are they similar? How are they different?

15. In another lifetime, could Summer have been a good person?

About the Author

Lyra R. Saenz is a writer of science fiction/fantasy. A romantic at heart with a love for supernatural horror, she believes that while happy endings don't come easily, they do come, even if it means excising your ex into a glass jar.

Born and raised in South Texas, Lyra is a multicultural, eyeliner–wielding member of the LGBTQ+ community, an animal–lover, and a cynic of all things political. She presently haunts the Houston area with her amazingly supportive partner and her feline–shaped void, Violet. Lyra grew up bouncing between her Chicano and Scandinavian heritages never feeling like she really fit in one world or the other.

Despite growing up on enchiladas and lefsa, she'll never turn down an offering of sushi or pho. And while her friends were getting boyfriends and girlfriends, she was too busy crushing on dreamy anime and manhwa characters to bother with real people. So, with one foot on either side of the border and her head full of East–Asian pop culture, she started creating her own worlds.

A lover of all things witchy, paranormal, and ghostly with a side of Victorian–futurism, cyberpunk, and posthumanism, Lyra imagines worlds where the IT tech is a werewolf, and the coffee machine has a fairy living inside it, but the androids love to take walks down the forest trail and host the occasional bonfire. When she isn't lost somewhere between an inkwell and a notebook, she can be found acting as a throne for the real queen of the household: her cat, and her royal majesty demands snuggles constantly. Or on calmer days, she'll sit and listen to her partner play video games while she unsuccessfully knits and/or binges her latest international tv show.

https://www.bookwitchsaenz.com/

Facebook: BookWitch.Saenz

Twitter: BookWitch_Saenz

Instagram: BookWitch_Saenz

BookWitchSaenz@gmail.com

Prelude

Falsetto in the Woods

Ragtime Swing

Sonata

Song of the Sea

The Devil's Trill

Bercuese

To Heal a Songbird

Ghost March

Nocturne

4 Horsemen Publications

Romance

Ann Shepphird

The War Council

Emily Bunney

All or Nothing
All the Way
All Night Long: Novella
All She Needs
Having it All
All at Once
All Together
All for Her

KT Bond

Back to Life
Back to Love
Back at Last

Lynn Chantale

The Baker's Touch
Blind Secrets
Broken Lens
Blind Fury
Time Bomb

VIP's Revenge
Chef's Taste

Mandy Fate

Love Me, Goaltender
Captain of My Heart

Mimi Francis

Private Lives
Private Protection
Private Party
Run Away Home
The Professor
Our Two-Week, One-Night Stand

Shae Coon

Bound in Love
Controlling Assets
For His Own Protection
Her Broken Pieces
The Roma's Claim
The Roma's Promise

Fantasy, SciFi, & Paranormal Romance

AMANDA FASCIANO

Waking Up Dead
Dead Vessel

BEAU LAKE

The Beast Beside Me
The Beast Within Me
Taming the Beast: Novella
The Beast After Me
Charming the Beast: Novella
The Beast Like Me
An Eye for Emeralds
Swimming in Sapphires
Pining for Pearls

CHELSEA BURTON DUNN

By Moonlight

DANIELLE ORSINO

Locked Out of Heaven
Thine Eyes of Mercy
From the Ashes
Kingdom Come
Fire, Ice, Acid, & Heart
A Fae is Done

J.M. PAQUETTE

Klauden's Ring
Solyn's Body
The Inbetween
Hannah's Heart

Call Me Forth
Invite Me In
Keep Me Close

JESSICA SALINA

Not My Time

KAIT DISNEY-LEUGERS

Antique Magic

LYRA R. SAENZ

Prelude
Falsetto in the Woods: Novella
Ragtime Swing
Sonata
Song of the Sea
The Devil's Trill
Bercuese
To Heal a Songbird
Ghost March
Nocturne

PAIGE LAVOIE

I'm in Love with Mothman

ROBERT J. LEWIS

Shadow Guardian and the
Three Bears

T.S. Simons

Antipodes
The Liminal Space
Ouroboros
Caim
Sessrúmnir
The 45th Parallel

Valerie Willis

Cedric: The Demonic Knight

Romasanta: Father of Werewolves
The Oracle: Keeper of the
Gaea's Gate
Artemis: Eye of Gaea
King Incubus: A New Reign

V.C. Willis

The Prince's Priest
The Priest's Assassin
The Assassin's Saint

Paranormal & Urban Fantasy

Amanda Fasciano

Waking Up Dead
Dead Vessel

Beau Lake

The Beast Beside Me
The Beast Within Me
Taming the Beast: Novella
The Beast After Me
Charming the Beast: Novella
The Beast Like Me
An Eye for Emeralds
Swimming in Sapphires
Pining for Pearls

Chelsea Burton Dunn

By Moonlight

J.M. Paquette

Call Me Forth
Invite Me In
Keep Me Close

Jessica Salina

Not My Time

Kait Disney-Leugers

Antique Magic

Lyra R. Saenz

Prelude
Falsetto in the Woods: Novella
Ragtime Swing
Sonata
Song of the Sea
The Devil's Trill
Bercuese

To Heal a Songbird
Ghost March
Nocturne

MEGAN MACKIE

The Saint Liars
The Devil's Day
The Finder of the Lucky Devil

PAIGE LAVOIE

I'm in Love with Mothman

ROBERT J. LEWIS

Shadow Guardian and the
Three Bears

VALERIE WILLIS

Cedric: The Demonic Knight
Romasanta: Father of Werewolves
The Oracle: Keeper of the
Gaea's Gate
Artemis: Eye of Gaea
King Incubus: A New Reign

FANTASY

D. LAMBERT

To Walk into the Sands
Rydan
Celebrant
Northlander
Esparan
King
Traitor
His Last Name

DANIELLE ORSINO

Locked Out of Heaven
Thine Eyes of Mercy
From the Ashes
Kingdom Come
Fire, Ice, Acid, & Heart
A Fae is Done

J.M. PAQUETTE

Klauden's Ring
Solyn's Body
The Inbetween
Hannah's Heart

LOU KEMP

The Violins Played Before Junstan
Music Shall Untune the Sky

R.J. YOUNG

Challenges of Tawa

VALERIE WILLIS

Cedric: The Demonic Knight
Romasanta: Father of Werewolves

The Oracle: Keeper of the
Gaea's Gate

Artemis: Eye of Gaea
King Incubus: A New Reign

Young Adult Fantasy

Blaise Ramsay

Through The Black Mirror
The City of Nightmares
The Astral Tower
The Lost Book of the Old Blood
Shadow of the Dark Witch
Chamber of the Dead God

Sins of The Father: Story of Silas
Honorable Darkness: Story of
Hex and Snip
A Love Lost: Story of Radnar

Leslie &
Janice Sommers

Brighde Reborn

C.R. Rice

Denial
Anger
Bargaining
Depression
Acceptance
Broken Beginnings:
Story of Thane
Shattered Start: Story of Sera

M.E. Batt

The Syphon's Daughter

Valerie Willis

Rebirth
Judgment
Death

Discover more at
4HorsemenPublications.com